THE TOFF PROCEEDS

The Toff Proceeds

JOHN CREASEY

Walker and Company • New York

Copyright © 1941, 1967 by John Creasey

All the characters and events portrayed in this
story are fictitious.

First published in the United States of America
in 1968 by Walker and Company, a division of
Walker Publishing Company, Inc.

Library of Congress Catalog Card Number:
68-13570.

Printed in the United States of America from
type set in Great Britain.

CHAPTER ONE

The Toff Says "Yes"

THERE was peace over the land and it was early summer. Winter had played its havoc and spring had put its soothing hand upon the earth, to bring forth flower and fruit and a new life in the fields and the hedgerows, to parkland and tiny cottage garden alike. The ramblers over many cottage doors were showing bursting buds of cream or white or pink or scarlet. The green of the meadows was soft and gentle, not yet parched for lack of rain. Quiet sounds of the country abounded, whisperings and muttering, the clanking of a horse-plough, the bustling flutter of the wings of ducks on the village pond as they washed and preened themselves.

It was a Thursday. No washing hung on the lines behind the cottages, and only one of the village's five shops was open.

Towards two o'clock two oldish men in yellow-white flannels and carrying a gaping cricket-bag between them strolled across the village green and, with great deliberation, stood by the darker, smoother patch in the middle, passing their opinion on the wicket for the afternoon's game. Soon others followed. A small hut, dark with a winter's coat of creosote, was opened. A little crowd of men applied themselves diligently to rolling the pitch selected for the game, which was between Fern Cross – the name of that village – and Appleby, a village five miles away. Both were part of the Crossfield estate, which stretched for many miles, and included three other villages and four farms, as well as coveys and copses, and large stretches of gorse and grassland,

7

which was left unfenced for the pleasure of the natives and the recreation of those holiday-makers who visited that little-known part of Surrey.

Fern Cross was tucked away between main roads, and the casual visitors were few. In it there had been no major scandal for twenty years. Rumours of war had reached the village, but of them little notice had been taken. War seemed a remote thing then, although the shadows were dark about the country.

Crime was as remote.

The shorter of the two men who had first reached the cricket green was Wally Simm, Fern Cross's one known criminal. He poached. Constable Thatcher, his next-door neighbour, played a strictly fair game with Wally, who was up before the local magistrates once a year, and always fined one pound.

This, then, was the extent of crime in Fern Cross. On the day when the match between the village and Appleby was due, an annual fixture likely to be fought out desperately, none knew or suspected the other shadow gathering about them.

For that matter, they did not know that the Crossfields' visitor that "week-end" was the Toff.

Had they done so few would have remembered what reputation the Toff had earned, although, since the daily papers reached the village regularly before twelve o'clock, those occasions when the Press had given him prominence must have reached their ears or their eyes.

They knew of him, variously, as Rawlinson, or Rollson, or Rolls or Rawlings, and none but the Crossfield household knew that he was, in fact, the Hon. Richard Rollison. The young Crossfields themselves were apt to scoff at Rollison's other life, and jokingly they called him their pet Jekyll and Hyde, since he was reputed to spend many of his nights in the East End of London, where it was said he was as well known as in the West End. Since he was eligible and a bachelor, good-looking and wealthy, and since he was supposed to be a most engaging conversationalist and one of the best after-dinner speakers in London, that was no small claim.

Mary Crossfield, tiny and pretty and twenty-one, laughed when she heard him spoken of as a criminologist and roundly declared that his East End jaunts were no more than pub-crawls of a dubious kind, and that he visited the district east of Aldgate Pump because he grew tired of the daily round in Mayfair and its environs. The Toff agreed that he grew tired of that. He rarely talked much to others about himself – or about his anti-criminal activities – and he had no objection to being derided.

That afternoon when Wally Simm was first on the cricket field Rollison was getting out his Frazer Nash to take Mary and Bill Crossfield to the green. Bill Crossfield was a good bat and a useful change bowler, who played for Fern Cross when he was at the Hall. Instead of finding Bill changed and ready for the game, Rollison found him scowling with the telephone in his hand. Ungraciously he said into it:

"Oh, all right. I'll come."

Bill was a man of medium height who looked less than his twenty-five years, hair brown and curly, eyes hazel and quick to smile or to condemn, impulsive, generous but spoiled. He slid his cigarette-case from his pocket and grunted.

"Of all the filthy luck. I was looking forward to the game no end."

"What's happened?" asked Rollison.

"*He* wants me to drive up to London at once. I wish to heaven I'd never allowed myself to get mixed up with the pesty company. Oh, well, it can't be helped. Mary" – his

9

sister was coming down the stairs, a dainty creature in a dress of cream silk, her auburn hair a fluffy halo about an elfin face – "tell Bramley I can't turn out, will you?"

Mary was startled.

"But, Bill, they're relying on you today."

"Well, it can't be helped. *He* wants me."

"Oh, *him*," said Mary disparagingly. "I wonder you take as much from him as you do."

Despite her words she made it clear that she knew there could be no appeal, and Rollison was puzzled – not for the first time since he had arrived on the previous evening for the "week-end" which, in the Crossfields' opinion, stretched from mid-week to mid-week. "He" and "him", pronouns used contemptuously or disdainfully, were frequently in the conversation. Rollison had gathered that Mary and Bill referred to Arnold Crossfield, their uncle; and he inferred also that although they had little respect for their uncle they deferred because he held the purse-strings.

After some hours he had discovered also that Bill and Mary lived with their mother at the Hall; that other relatives came and went at will, freely accepting the Crossfields' extravagant hospitality, but that Arnold rarely visited the Hall except at Christmas or, as Mary put it, some occasion when he would put a damper on high spirits.

Rollison, who had never met Arnold Crossfield, imagined him as a middle-aged, humourless and earnest man, and thought privately that Bill would certainly be the better for a little discipline. Bill had recently taken an active interest in the Crossfield Manufacturing Company, and found that it demanded far more of his time than he had expected. Clearly Uncle Arnold had held out some threat, probably of a reduced allowance out of the estate, to enforce obedience.

They were the circumstances, then, which led to Rollison

10

driving only Mary to the village. There the two teams were having a practice knock before the toss for the first innings on a wicket almost as perfect as it looked; there were no plantains or bad patches on the Fern Cross pitch.

Two men, Wally Simm and Bramley – the Fern Cross captain – strolled towards the car. Wally was of medium height and weather-beaten, a countryman with a slow gait but a surprisingly cunning right hand which could spin the ball both ways. Bramley was a tall, clean-cut, middle-aged man, a retired soldier who nursed and drilled the side as he would a regiment.

"Hallo, Mary, where's Bill?"

"He can't come."

"Can't . . ." Bramley's expression, cordial enough until then, changed ludicrously. "But that's absurd. we're relying on him."

"He didn't know until the last minute. It was an urgent call from London," said Mary. "I'm sorry, but –"

"Sorry!" muttered Bramley. He met Rollison's glance full of sympathy for a captain who was let down at the last moment by one of his star players.

"We're going to get a trouncing," Bramley said gloomily. "Defoe hasn't turned up, either. Of course he's always un- reliable, but –" he shrugged.

"Mr. Defoe told me he would come, sure," declared Wally Simm.

"Yes, but that was last week –"

"No, it weren't," declared Wally flatly. "Last night it were. Late," he added with finality. "Just druv up, he had, from Lunnon. " 'Allo,' he ses to me, 'what are you doin' out at this time o'night, you old scoundrel?' 'Mindin' me own,' I ses, 'like most folk ought to.' He laughed – he's a rare one for a laugh, he is – laughed, he did, and ses: 'Well, I've come back for this precious game tomorrow. Doan' stay out late enough to get that wrist of yours stiff.' "

Wally delivered this statement in a low-pitched and monotonous voice, having finished he stared at Rollison, continuing to do so while Bramley went across to the other members of the team. A twelfth man had put in an appearance, so that Fern Cross could field ten men. The eleventh, it appeared, would not turn up.

It was Mary who said, just before Bramley tossed a coin with the opposing skipper:

"Why don't you ask Mr. Rollison to play?"

Bramley looked uncertain.

"A risky thing to suggest," Rollison murmured.

"Er – do you play?" asked Bramley.

"A bit," said the Toff, who was often deceptively modest.

"Tommy's boots would fit you, he's got large feet," said Mary unkindly. "I can hop back for them. Is it all right?" she asked Bramley, and the captain nodded, giving the impression that he knew he would have to hide Rollison in the field, but that anyone was better than no eleventh man at all.

He lost the toss.

For the first fifteen minutes Rollison stood idly on the outfield while the Appleby opening pair sedulously dug themselves in, as if this were a whole-day match and not a half-day frolic. Rollison, to whom cricket was a minor religion, was amused and yet on the whole glad that he was playing. He hoped Mary would arrive with Bill's spiked boots before he had any sprinting to do, but it was not so.

A lofty hit some fifteen yards from him made him hurry and he was within reach of the catch when his shiny-soled shoes slipped on the grass, consequently he missed it. He heard a groan from a near-by fieldsman, someone said "bad luck" half-heartedly, Bramley glared, and Rollison smarted

12

- as all men who know that they have been unfairly judged will smart on a cricket field.

Mary then brought the boots, which fitted; they were no more than tens.

Rollison was able to put them on when, with the score at twenty-four, an Appleby batsman hit across a leg-break from Wally, and heard his bails fall. The game took a livelier turn, for the next batsman was a powerful hitter, and kept the ball down. As the score mounted quickly into the fifties, the Toff grew hot with unaccustomed running in the deep, for usually he fielded first or second slip. Then his fortune changed, for the big hitter lifted one a little, driving it with considerable force. The Toff took it shoulder high.

"Oh, good *catch*!" cried Bramley, and after strolling towards him: "You don't bowl, I suppose?"

"Only straight up-and-down," said Rollison.

"That might be useful if we go on like this," said Bramley. "They've a powerful batting side. I shall be darned glad to get them out for a hundred and fifty."

It looked as if he would have cause to be glad, and, actually, Appleby scored five less than two hundred, the speed of the batting improving after the first three-quarters of an hour. At half past four they were all out, and in the tea interval Bramley elected to sit next to Rollison, whom he had not called on to bowl.

"You did some good work in the deep," he said appreciatively. "Where do you usually bat?"

"Oh, I don't mind," said Rollison.

"No, give me a straight answer. Defoe would have opened for us – he's the best bat we've had on this green for a long time; odd fellow, but a damned good cricketer. If you care to open – no one else wants to – you won't be putting anyone out. Will you?"

"If you say so," agreed the Toff. "I'll enjoy it, I hope."

13

The afternoon grew warmer, and a crowd of over a hundred people gathered after tea, nearly half of them from Appleby. Appleby considered the game in the bag, for without Defoe and Crossfield no one thought that Fern Cross could muster much more than a hundred. The sight of Rollison in light grey flannels, borrowed boots, and a pair of pads a little too short for his long legs did not inspire them with misgivings. Nor did Rollison's third stroke, a turn to leg which sent the ball skimming to the boundary.

There was polite clapping from the corner beneath some oak trees which served as a pavilion.

Then Rollison, who had played many seasons for Norfolk and was a Cambridge blue, during which period he had been adjudged the best University batsman in the country – began to enjoy himself. Appleby's bowling was steady, but not brilliant, and after ten minutes the Toff was seeing the ball well enough to talk to it before deciding what to do. The easy mastery of his strokes took the players and spectators by surprise. Then Fern Cross realized that it was not luck, and began to cheer.

With the score at a hundred and thirty, and Rollison's share eighty-one, he hit a spinner too soon, and a lanky Appleby mid-on flung himself at the ball to make a catch which brought the house down. Two wickets had fallen before Rollison's, but Fern Cross did not betray the start he had given them, and he found himself the centre of an admiring team who declared that Defoe could not have done better, if as well. Fern Cross passed the Appleby total with seven wickets down, and, as is the way of village cricketers in the south, went on to score two hundred and forty before allowing the perspiring and disgruntled Appleby eleven a respite.

Bramley might have been a friend of long standing, so loyally did he stay by Rollison, and so eagerly did he urge his find to have a drink at the Fern Cross Inn before going back to the Hall. The two teams foregathered, and the game was discussed from every angle, the one thing on which all agreed being the brilliance of the newcomer's innings. Rollison turned the conversation towards Defoe.

Bramley and Wally Simm were with him.

Bramley frowned.

"Defoe's a fine bat – no doubt about that at all. And he can send 'em down when he's in the right mood. But he's the most unreliable beggar imaginable. He lives on his own in a little cottage on the borders of the parish – spends half his time there, and half in London. It's nothing to have a wire from him on the morning of a game, saying he can't come."

Rollison played with the handle of a pewter tankard.

"He does take the trouble to send a wire?"

"Oh yes. He's keen enough in his way, but –" Bramley shrugged in the manner of a man who considers cricket first and everything else also-ran, while the Toff added thoughtfully:

"Yet he didn't send a message today?"

"He was probably drunk," said Bramley.

"He came down from London late last night for the game, Wally says." Simm was 'Wally' to all-comers very quickly.

"That 'e did," declared Wally in his inimitable monotonous voice. " 'Mind you get that pitch true's a billiard-table,' he ses to me, 'I feel like a hunner'd.' I'm goin' straight over there, that's what I be doing, to see he's all right." Wally drained his tankard and refused another, while Rollison said:

"I'll drive you, Wally."

"I got me legs," said Wally dourly. "Miss Mary will be coming back, won't she?"

"No," said the Toff. Mary had gone off at tea, saying

that if she were not back by six o'clock she wouldn't be back at all. "Coming, Bramley?"

"Great Scott, no I can't see why you're so interested." Rollison smiled.

"I'm curious by nature," he said, and then followed Wally outside. The poacher climbed into the small car with the attitude of a man suspicious of automobiles, and when the Toff settled down at the wheel the countryman said:

"Up to the crossroads, an' then right, an' then left – take the fork and go straight along. The left fork," he added hastily. "I don't bide wi' talkin' to anyone when he's driving, an' I never will."

"A very fine principle," approved Rollison, and for the next ten minutes, while he followed Wally's directions faithfully, he pondered over Defoe. Rollison had called himself curious by nature, which was true. He had an instinct for oddity, and he could not understand why a cricketer who took the trouble to wire when he could not play, who returned to Fern Cross specially for a game, and thus was obviously very keen, should not turn up or send a message.

His curiosity, nevertheless, was comparatively mild. Had Wally not been so talkative, had Defoe not been made out so unreliable and contradictory a character, he would not have troubled to make the journey. He might even have gone back to London knowing little or nothing of what happened in the small cottage where Defoe spent half of his time.

But he did go: and so, for him, the case began.

CHAPTER TWO

Discovery at the Cottage

THE cottage was set in the midst of a clearing, a picturesque setting with a background of pine and oak trees, with some patches of heatherland about it. A charming place, buried in the heart of Surrey, some half a mile from the nearest road; it was approached from Wally's 'fork' by a cart-track.

The wicket-gate was open, and swaying gently in the wind.

"That's odd," said the Toff.

"Ay," declared Wally. "Not often he leaves that open, or lets others."

The oddness which the Toff saw would have struck very few people. He noticed it because the lawns and the ramblers, the garden and the cottage itself, were so trim and neat and well cared for that it seemed wrong for the gate to be left carelessly off its catch.

"Who does the garden?" he inquired.

"What I don't do, he does," said Wally.

"Oh, you work for him?"

"I do 'is heavy work," said Wally reluctantly. "Always found him a fair-dealing gentleman, an' I don't care what anyone else says." He ended on a note of defiance, as if challenging the Toff to ask what others said.

"It's a good working principle, Wally."

"Some people –" hinted Wally darkly.

He did not go on, and the Toff, although curious about the manner of life which Defoe led – one which obviously called for criticism in the village – pulled up close to the

17

swaying wicket-gate. Wally climbed out, shook himself as if to get rid of the contamination of the car, and waited for Rollison to enter the garden.

It was not one which grew less pleasant on close inspection. The lawns were as trim as they had seemed from a distance, and the rich brown earth of the flower-beds had been hoed recently. So recently, in fact, that there was a light dry film on the top of some of the beds – newly turned damp earth which had dried when exposed to the sun.

"Did you work here this morning?" Rollison asked.

"No, Mondays an' Wednesdays I'm here." Wally looked sideways. "Why did you ask un, sir?"

"Someone's been busy in the last hour or two," said the Toff.

Into Wally's eyes there appeared something akin to respect.

"Not many Londoners would ha' seen that."

"Not all Londoners are strangers to the country," smiled the Toff. "And we do have gardens in London, Wally."

"Gardens – uh."

"And good ones," insisted the Toff as they reached the front door. "But it makes it look more curious, doesn't it? If he had time to garden, he had time to play cricket."

Wally grunted again, and tapped on the front door, which had no knocker. It was of oak, well oiled and healthy-looking. The letter-box and the iron of the keyhole were painted a dull black, and there were bolt heads showing.

There was no answer.

A fresh wind sang across the garden, bringing with it the perfume of flowers and new-cut grass, and a faint sighing sound, which mingled with the trilling of birds. That was all. Wally doubled a gnarled fist and thumped on the door, but he had no answer.

He tried the latch.

The door did not open, and he looked sideways again.

"Maybe he's round the back," he said, and led the way.

Behind the cottage, and with tall trees growing about it, was a small timber-built garage. One door stood ajar, and the Toff glanced in, to see a small car – a ten or twelve horse-power – standing there. It was black or dark blue, with a red line running about the coachwork.

"What car does he run, Wally?"

"One o' they M.G.'s," said Wally disparagingly, and looked into the garage. "That's it. So he should be in."

"Ye-es." They reached the back door, and repeated the earlier performance at the font. There was no response, but this time when the latch was lifted the door opened. Wally poked his head in and shouted:

"*Mis*-ter – *De*-foe!"

The two words echoed about a small, well-kept kitchen, but again there was no answer. Wally pushed out his lips, and regarded the Toff uncertainly.

"It's a queer set up," he declared.

"He could have gone for a walk."

"Ay. But why didn't he come to the game, that's what I want to know? It aren't like him, that's a fact, sir. It aren't like him to miss playing if he's here – comes from London speshul I'm aware, an' more than once. Garden's been worked, door's open, car's in the garage. If you ask me, I don't understand it."

"What do we do?" asked Rollison. "Go in?"

"We could," said Wally slowly, "but I don't say he would like it if he copped us." Thus speaking, Wally stepped across the threshold, and the Toff followed him, driven on by a curiosity which had grown strong enough for him to risk any minor difference with the owner – or tenant – if he returned from a walk. Rollison was assuring himself that the obvious solution was the right one, and that for private

19

reasons Defoe had decided not to play. He might have received an unexpected visitor, and it would not be easy for him to send a message to the green. Everything considered, thought Rollison, he was behaving in a manner at once reprehensible and childish.

Wally opened a door leading to a narrow passage. A glow of daylight came from the far end, but the front door was not in sight. Nevertheless, as Wally stepped to the passage, a door closed.

Not loudly, nor clearly.

The soft *click* of a latch had a stealthy note, and the sharper dropping of the latch afterwards echoed loudly. Wally started, and the Toff turned about.

"I'll have a look at the front again, Wally – you stay where you are."

It was his habit to act quickly, and at times to jump to conclusions. Now, he jumped to one; that someone had been in the cottage all the time, but had preferred not to answer the knock – and the same someone, finding that the callers were coming in at the back door, was going out by the front.

He moved very quickly, and he reached the side of the house in time to see a girl near the wicket-gate.

She was half-running, and she ran gracefully. As she reached the gate, she looked over her shoulder, and saw Rollison. 'Half' no longer described her running, for she took to her heels, and covered the ten yards between the gate and Rollison's car very quickly.

Rollison tucked his elbows into his sides and he too ran in earnest. As he did so he saw her hesitate by the car. The hesitation was not long-lived, for she pulled open the door and slipped into the driving-seat.

Rollison had left the ignition key in the dashboard.

He did not waste time in shouting, but drew a deeper

20

breath and ran as fast as he knew how. The engine started smoothly, and the girl showed that she was used to handling a Frazer Nash for she started off at once. She might have got clear away but for the fact that she did not see a small ditch just ahead of her and the nearside wheel slipped into it.

The engine stalled.

Rollison reached the gate and vaulted over. He had ten yards to cover while the girl restarted the engine. She had succeeded by the time the Toff reached the back of the car, and she accelerated so sharply that the lurch almost shook him off when he leapt on the side. But he held on, as the girl set the wheels to the cart-track and opened out.

The Toff climbed into the rear seat.

She must have seen him in the driving-mirror, for her hands left the wheel for a moment, and her foot came off the accelerator.

"Treat it more gently," urged the Toff, and he climbed over the back of the seat next to hers. She let the engine stall again, and sat quite still, looking ahead. The Toff was a little out of breath and more than a little puzzled, but neither factor was enough to make him ignore a pretty girl when he saw one.

'Pretty' was only half-true.

With a slightly longer nose and longer upper-lip she might have been called beautiful. If she just missed that – and he was a connoisseur – she was certainly very lovely, and there was a defiant lift to her chin as she stared ahead. A small hat did not properly control her hair, some of which, dark brown, had worked loose. She had very long, dark lashes.

"After all," went on the Toff when he had recovered his breath, "cars are like children, they need handling. This one has never let me down yet, but I can't be sure that it never will."

Her lips parted, and she drew a deep breath.

"What are you going to do?"

"I don't know," admitted the Toff. "I think we should go into a huddle about it. I'm not a positive stickler to convention, and if you had a really good reason I shouldn't complain about you borrowing my car."

"What right have you got to ask for explanations?"

She turned to face him; her profile had not belied her looks, and angry blue eyes stared into his. She had an oval face, and her chin was pointed.

"Well, it *is* my car," said the Toff mildly. He contemplated her leisurely, and began to take out his cigarette-case. "On the whole I think that gives me right enough. Will you smoke?"

She ignored the suggestion, and her breathing grew quicker. He knew that there was more than anger in her eyes; she was afraid, and he wanted to know what caused her fear. Beyond that he had few ideas, for he had not properly adjusted himself to the situation.

He thought that she was going to speak, but she did not get the words out before a cry came from the cottage. He looked over his shoulder and he saw Wally standing in the doorway, waving somewhat wildly. Gradually his words reached Rollison.

"Get a doctor! Get – a – doctor!"

The girl heard also, and the colour drained from her face.

CHAPTER THREE

The Reluctant Lady

ROLLISON was in a quandary. Wally was not a man likely to get easily excited, and his shout held an urgent note which

22

made the need for a doctor imperative, Rollison, on the other hand, wanted to talk to the girl, who was not likely to talk willingly.

He said: "I think I'll drive."

"What are you going to do?" she demanded.

"Get a doctor," said Rollison. "Do you know of one near here?"

"No."

"Then we'll have to drive to the village." He slipped out of his seat and walked to the other side of the car, expecting her to make a rush away from him. Perhaps she knew that she could not get far, for she slid into the seat he had left, making no attempt to go, and doing nothing to interfere with him as he slipped in the clutch and started off.

He was half-way along the road to Fern Cross when he saw three men cycling towards him, all in white flannels. The cricketers had come from the inn, their celebrating at an end. They recognized him as he slowed down, and three browned faces broke into wide grins, quickly suppressed.

"I'm afraid we're in trouble," said Rollison. "A doctor is needed at Mr. Defoe's house. Where's the nearest one?"

A little man who had shown surprising hitting powers answered immediately.

"Dr. Whittaker, sir, in the village."

"He's in, I just see him in the garden," said another.

"Good. How long would it take one of you to fetch him?"

"No more'n five minutes," said the little man, immediately turning his bicycle. "Mr. Defoe's cottage. I'll tell him, sir. George, you let the missus know I'm likely to be late," he added, and started off at a good speed. The others showed some inclination to linger, but Rollison gave them no encouragement. He waved as, drawing ahead, he moved the car on to the cart-track.

All the time the girl at his side had kept silent. The men

23

had eyed her with frank curiosity, and he could not prevent himself from associating her with the life that Defoe led – a life not considered irreproachable from village standards. The track led through common-land, with gorse and fern on either side, and there was a view for several miles in one direction, although in another it was broken by a line of tall pine trees.

The girl was staring towards the trees.

Rollison kept silent, watching her out of the corner of his eyes. Now that the doctor was being summoned he had no particular object in returning to the cottage quickly, much though he wanted to find out what had happened and what had so disturbed Wally. The obvious probability was that Defoe was ill, or had been hurt.

He saw the girl's gloved hand playing with the handle of the door.

She was dressed in a brown tweed suit, and wore thin gloves of tan colour. Her hands and feet were long and slim; one of the county, he reflected, not of the village.

He slowed down deliberately, nearing a bend.

She saw what she thought was her chance, and opened the door. The Toff braked so suddenly that the jerk threw her off balance, and before she was out of the car his left hand gripped her wrist. She squirmed round and struck at him with her free hand. The blow did no more than ruffle his dark hair.

"That's not friendly," he said, and his grip tightened. "Don't try to get away. You'll hurt yourself."

"Why don't you let me go?"

"I don't know that you deserve to go."

She stopped struggling. He did not start the engine again, and she said in a muffled voice:

"Let me go, please. No one – no one need know you did; I might have slipped away."

"Not from me," said Rollison.

"Who the devil do you think you are?"

"I don't think we need start a slanging match. Supposing you tell me what you were doing in Defoe's cottage?"

She tightened her lips and her chin went up.

"All right," he said resignedly, "tell me what happened there, if the motive of your visit doesn't bear investigation."

She coloured furiously.

"I'm doing a reasonable best to make you say something that's sensible," Rollison went on.

"I – I've nothing to say."

"Quite a reluctant lady, aren't you?" said the Toff. "You were reluctant to be seen, and reluctant to stay; now you're reluctant to talk. But you'll have to talk, sooner or later. There could be more unreasonable listeners than I."

"It's got nothing to do with you."

The Toff considered carefully.

"I don't know that you're right. Every citizen is concerned with crime – or an act against the law."

She turned sharply in her seat, her eyes blazing.

"What do you mean by crime?"

"The word is fairly well known," said the Toff mildly. "It seems to have touched a tender spot, too. But supposing I put it in a different way? Have you or have you not done anything which might be considered law-breaking? I don't mean trespass," he added, and she drew a deep breath.

"You're simply laughing at me! Of all the beastly individuals –"

Rollison shrugged. "If you were wise you'd have that cigarette, and try to think and talk more rationally. You're letting off steam, and you're badly frightened. It's a frame of mind which might get you into trouble." He offered her a cigarette, and this time she took one, although there was

25

reluctance about her movement. He lit it, and one for himself, and then said abruptly:

"How badly was Defoe hurt?"

He scored easily there, for she started and her eyes showed bewilderment as well as fear.

"How did you know he was hurt?"

"I inferred it," said Rollison, and did not let her realize that she had told him indirectly that there was no question of illness. He was brisk as he went on: "Can I do anything for him, do you think?"

"I – I don't know. He's unconscious. I – I stopped the bleeding by padding it up." She spoke very quickly and in an undertone, as if speaking to herself. "I didn't do it, you must believe me, I went there to see him, and I found him lying on the floor. But they mustn't know I was there. They mustn't, do you understand?"

"Yes, of course," said Rollison soothingly. "And I don't see why they should. Would anyone about here recognize you?"

"Who – who do you mean?"

"The men we met on the road, for instance?"

"No, of course not. I'm only known at –" She stopped, and stared at him. "Who are you? Why are you asking all these questions? Why haven't you sent for the police, why –"

"Now who's asking the questions?" demanded Rollison. "What's your name?"

"I –"

"It's just possible that I can help you," Rollison went on, "but if you're going to keep on acting like a sulky schoolgirl, you're past help. I should be in the cottage, seeing what I can do. If I go there I can't trust you to tell me your right name, or to wait for me. I can only give the police a full and accurate description of you, if you run away." He knew

26

that he was taking a considerable chance when he reached his decision, but he was aching to get to the cottage before the doctor arrived. "Is that clear?"

"I – I thought you said you might help me."

"Provided you stay near at hand until I'm through at the cottage, I will – if I can," he said. "If you're missing when I come out, I can't – and I shan't try. I shall give your description to the police, and leave it at that." He began to move the car forward, and in a few seconds was in sight of the cottage, although trees growing near hid the car from the view of anyone there. "Will you wait?"

It was difficult to read her expression; the fear remained, but there was also hope and bewilderment. But she answered 'Yes' promptly enough.

"All right, slip out here," said Rollison. "And, please – don't prove me wrong."

"In what?" She was half-way out of the car.

"In taking you on trust."

He drove more quickly as soon as she was on the grass verge and heading for the trees, and he did not look back. He was afraid that he was wrong, yet the urge to see what had happened to Defoe was too strong to be resisted. It was his habit to take chances, and that was one of the things of which the police complained, often bitterly. He admitted that there were times when he treated the authorities in too cavalier a fashion, but as often declared that they invited it.

He drew up nearer to the gate this time, and within three minutes of leaving the girl he was inside the cottage. Wally had left the door open. He was bending over a couch in a room to the right of the small hall.

Lying on the couch was a good-looking man with raven-black hair. He had on white flannel trousers and brown shoes. By the couch was a pair of cricket boots, and leaning

27

against the wall a cricket bag with the white of pads showing through the opening, which was drawn together by leather straps.

Those things the Toff saw at once.

Just as quickly he saw that the man's shirt was off, and that he was stripped to the waist. Blood showed on his chest, where it had seeped from beneath a padded cloth, which looked like a pillow-case. Defoe's face was a deathly white; against it, Wally's tanned skin was almost black.

"Well, Wally?" said Rollison.

"There's nothing to be done 'fore doctor arrives," said Wally Simm clearly. "Someone's patched he up, for sure."

"What have you done?"

"Nothing," said Wally. "There weren't nothing to do, sir. I've just sat and watched him – wetting his lips with water; they do say spirits isn't a thing to give when a man's been hurt."

"Playing for safety is quite right," said Rollison, and he felt Defoe's pulse. It was weak, but gave no suggestion of failing altogether. "Who took off his shirt?"

"It wasn't me," said Wally.

"Have you touched anything?"

"I aren't a fool," said Wally gruffly. "I touched nothing, an' " – he turned his berry-brown eyes on the Toff and added carefully – "I bain't seen nothing, sir. That's me. I see nothing, not if anyone asks me about a young lady." He wiped his hand across his mouth as if to give further emphasis to his words while the Toff eyed him, wondering whether Wally Simm could be relied on to maintain that attitude, at least until he – the Toff – had been able to talk to the girl.

He was deliberating on what next to say when he heard a car draw up outside. He stepped to the window and saw the little cyclist climbing out of a big Austin, followed by

28

a portly, grey-haired and hatless man carrying a small case. He took a chance then, and said:

"You're quite right, Wally. We saw nothing – or rather you didn't. If there's trouble coming, I'll take it. I'd rather like to help that girl."

The berry-brown eyes stared at him.

"What girl, sir?" asked Wally Simm, as footsteps drew near to the cottage.

CHAPTER FOUR

Interval with Iris

ROLLISON had seen many doctors examining an injured man; his acquaintance with the routine following murder and other deeds of violence was of long standing. His experience was that fifty per cent of the doctors were too fussy, forty per cent too perfunctory – at the first examination, at least, and often because they preferred not to give a definite opinion – and ten per cent were just right.

Dr. Whittaker belonged to the last category.

He said 'Good evening' to Rollison but spared him, and Wally, only a glance. He put his bag down, and said: "Get me some hot water, please."

Wally went immediately to the kitchen, while Whittaker removed the compress.

"Who put this on?" he asked.

"I don't know," said Rollison; his first lie.

"Hmmm. Made a good job of it, at all events. One good thing, most people are familiar with elementary first aid these days. It should be made a compulsory subject at schools, I think." Whittaker took Defoe's temperature, grunted, tried his pulse and frowned, and then examined

29

the wound, which was high in the left breast.

That was the moment the Toff had been wanting.

The wound was some inch wide, and little more than a sixteenth of an inch thick. That thickness was mostly caused by the swelling about it; the flesh close to the cut was discoloured, and dried blood was about that. There were no other marks of violence on a creamy-coloured, healthy-looking chest.

"*Hum*," said Dr. Whittaker with emphasis, and turned to look squarely at Rollison for the first time. "We'll have to have the police along quickly. Would you mind going for them?"

"I'll send for them," promised Rollison. "What about the back of the head – concussion from a blow, do you think?"

Whittaker turned and raised Defoe's head gently. The Toff saw a slight swelling, and was wondering whether the blow had been delivered before or after the knife wound. He thought the latter; had Defoe been knocked unconscious first, whoever had stabbed him would have made sure that the stab was a fatal one. At least that premise seemed reasonable. The blow, he thought, was an accidental one, made when Defoe had fallen after the attack.

"Hum-*hum*," said Whittaker. "Ye-es, that could be. Considerable blood lost, too – that would induce unconsciousness. He wasn't found on the couch, was he?"

"He was there when I arrived. Why?"

Whittaker regarded him with one eyebrow raised above the other; a humorous, likeable man, whose eyes were remarkably clear and blue.

"Come," he said, "you deduced the bump on the head, but you didn't notice that there's no blood to speak of on the couch?"

Rollison smiled, apologetically.

"There can be two opinions, you know. Is there anything I can do before sending for the police and having a look round?"

"Not for me, once I get that hot water," said Whittaker. "A pity he didn't have the telephone fixed, wasn't it? Ah, come on Simm, we can't wait all day."

There was no need to worry about Defoe now that Whittaker was in charge, and Rollison went out. The little cyclist was in the kitchen, putting on another kettle of water – there was an electric stove. Rollison found him eager to hurry to the police, and advised him to ask the local constable to telephone the Surrey Headquarters at once. When the man was on his way he returned to the front room.

For the first time he was able to look at the furniture.

It was of good quality, the modern electric fitments and an electric fire well chosen. The floor was covered with rugs and mats, all of skin. The boards themselves were polished a dark colour, but near the window there was a large damp patch. One light-coloured rug was also damp. He finished examining the patch, and then looked through the other rooms – four in all. The dining-room and main bedroom were quietly furnished, the general effect pleasing. One of the spare rooms was furnished as a library; a light, airy, pleasant room. The last was another bedroom, small, indeed barely large enough for its single suite of furniture and a modern divan bed. There were patterned chintzes at the windows, on the bedside chair, the eiderdown and the coverlet. At a guess he would have declared it a woman's room.

There was much to puzzle him, but there were things which spoke for themselves. Defoe was a man of taste, and one who did not need to watch his expenses too closely. The garden showed the same liberality and the same care. He wondered who looked after the inside of the cottage, and decided to inquire of Wally; but first he wanted to see the girl.

He looked in on Whittaker.

"Will you be here when the police arrive?"

"Yes – won't you?" Whittaker was not a man likely to mince words.

"I'll be round and about," smiled Rollison. "Presumably someone came here to do this, and there might be signs of their presence outside."

"I think you'd better let me have your card," said Whittaker, laconically.

"Of course." Rollison took a card from his wallet. "If you do need to get in touch with me, I'm staying at Crossfield Hall."

"Oh – that's all right." Mention of the Hall apparently relieved Whittaker of anxiety. Rollison smiled as he went out, and strolled towards the gate. He made a considerable show of examining the lawn on either side of the path, and the patch of sandy earth outside the garden. Then he walked, still slowly, towards the belt of trees where the girl should be waiting.

By then he was prepared to find that he had been a fool; he did not really expect to find her.

He reached the trees, and went to the other side. There was a queer mixture of disappointment and expectancy inside him, and he was startled when a voice said softly:

"I'm here."

He turned on his heel.

The girl had been sitting on the stump of a tree, one which was nearly surrounded by hawthorn bushes; she had not taken any chances of being seen by passers-by.

"I was just telling myself that you'd gone," Rollison admitted.

"If I had, the police would have been hunting for me," she said bitterly.

Rollison sat down on a patch of grass not far from her, and motioned to the tree stump.

The girl remained standing, staring down at him.

"What *are* you doing?"

"Trying to honour my promise to help if I could," said Rollison. His smile clearly reassured her, for she sank down beside him.

"May I have a cigarette?"

He supplied one, and lit it.

"That's better," he said. "And now don't you think we should get acquainted? My name is Rollison, temporarily at Crossfield Hall, permanently at 55g Gresham Terrace, W.1." He spoke easily, and after he had said 'Crossfield Hall' he did not change the tone or tempo of his voice, although he saw the slight, involuntary movement, and wondered why mention of the Hall should cause it. He hoped that she would tell him; instead:

"Must we exchange names?"

"I can't help you if you stay anonymous."

"How *can* you help me?"

"So far I'm doing pretty well," the Toff pointed out. "Instead of handing you over to the police for inquiries I've not only kept you away from anyone, but persuaded the other man who saw you that he didn't. No, don't start saying 'thanks'. It's as much for myself as for you."

"For yourself?"

"That's what I said," said Rollison patiently. "Odd though it seems, my side-line is crime. People have heard of me, and the Press has occasionally fallen over itself with enthusiasm. But you wouldn't read the papers."

"I can't remember – Rollison, did you say?"

He smiled.

33

"There's some foolish nickname, which might strike a chord. The Toff. Toffee without the double 'e'."

It was one of the few occasions when he blessed newspaper publicity, for she recognized him as the Toff where she had not as Rollison. She stared at him, her cigarette neglected, her eyes widening, her breathing coming much more quickly. She was finding it hard to believe – tremendously glad, as anyone in her plight might be, since the Toff had been dubbed a modern Robin Hood, a twentieth-century knight-errant, and other such romantic things.

She said: "Oh no, it's not possible!"

"Quite seriously, it's true," said Rollison. "And I'd like to do what I can. After all, it has all the elements of an intriguing problem. Defoe is badly hurt, and was hurt between one-thirty and one-forty-five. You arrived some time after that, probably about seven o'clock. Between your arrival at seven and his injury, someone did some gardening. No, don't echo *gardening!*' It won't contribute to the problem: The seven o'clock visit *was* your second, wasn't it? You've committed one serious breach of moral duty if nothing else. After you first found him, you should have sent for a doctor. Why didn't you?"

She swallowed hard.

"How – how on earth do you know when I came? And when he was attacked?"

"If it will simplify things, I'll tell you. He was dressed and ready for the game this afternoon. Being keen, he would be at the green in good time, so he wouldn't leave here later than one-forty-five for a two o'clock start. So whoever used the knife was here after he had changed – which he wouldn't be likely to do until after lunch – and before one-forty-five. That settles item one. You arrived when the wound was bleeding, and you put on a compress. Had the seven o'clock visit been your first, the bleeding would have been stopped for some time. So you dressed the wound, and went away. Of course you might have stayed, but I can't imagine you spending the whole afternoon there. You didn't, did you?"

"No-o. I – I came back -"

"To look for something. Letters?" asked the Toff.

"No."

He frowned. "I rather expected it to be letters. But before we go on to that, what is your name?"

She answered promptly enough then.

"Brent – Iris Brent."

"Well now, you did make the two visits, and so you did want something. And you must have realized that Defoe needed medical attention. What sent you away?"

She said very slowly:

"*They* came back."

"Who are 'they'?"

"I don't know. The – the people who attacked him, I suppose. I – I'll tell you just what happened. I came to see him. I had to see him on important personal business. I got here just after two o'clock, and I found him lying – lying by the window, bleeding badly. I've been through a first-aid course, so I started to do what I could. I took a pillow-case from the airing-cupboard, bathed the wound and made a compress, bandaging it tightly to stop the bleeding. As I'd come along the road I'd seen three men going away from the cottage. I didn't know them, I only noticed them vaguely. Then, when I'd been here half an hour, they came back. I slipped out the back way, and waited here. I don't think they knew where I was; they didn't look for me. When they'd gone, I went back. Soon afterwards you arrived. I – I haven't been so frightened in my life."

Rollison chuckled.

"I can imagine. If I'm to help – and with that story you're

35

going to need help – I should know everything about it, shouldn't I?"

"Yes." She stood up from the tree-trunk. "I can trust you, and I must, but it's so difficult –" She paused. In the distance a car changed gear, and Rollison guessed that the police were on the way; he had been talking with or looking for Iris Brent for nearly half an hour, and the little cricketer had been gone for three-quarters. "Can't I tell you somewhere else? I'm scared here."

"I think the quicker the better," said Rollison.

It was then, quite unexpectedly, that he heard footsteps near by. They came so suddenly that on the instant he knew that someone had been watching and listening, someone not ten yards away. He turned abruptly – and a man came in sight, a tall, very pale-faced man, who was holding an automatic pistol in his right hand.

CHAPTER FIVE

Unpleasant for the Toff

THE surprise of the encounter worried the Toff more than the threat of the gun. That the other could have been near at hand for some time, without being suspected, was a galling thought. It was useless to tell himself that he had no reason at all for suspecting the presence; he should be prepared for all eventualities, and from the moment Iris Brent had talked of three men the warning should have been in letters of red against his mind.

As it was, he had to face the unexpected.

He put one hand to his pocket, and the man snapped: "Keep your hands in sight!"

"Oh," said the Toff, "then you *are* serious."

"I'm serious, and you'll know it before I've finished." The

36

voice was rough, but nevertheless suggested an educated man. The cut of dark grey flannels was good, and the one thing unusual about the wearer was his almost bleached skin – not a transparent whiteness, such as comes from some illnesses or conditions of the blood, but a dull pallor. But for that he would have been good-looking. His cheek-bones were high, his eyes a little narrow, and he had a nose slightly broad at the nostrils; in him there was a strain of Mongol or Chinese blood, thought Rollison.

The car drew nearer to the belt of trees.

If he shouted then he could attract attention; if he kept quiet he would avoid the risk of a shot from the automatic, but he might find it impossible to turn the tables. He was deliberating when he looked at Iris; the colour had ebbed from her cheeks, leaving her as pale as their assailant.

He had seen her frightened – but not so frightened as she was now.

She started:

"Put – put that gun –"

"You keep quiet!" The man's voice was low and threatening. At the same moment the police car passed. The moment for calling gone with it. "Sam, put him out."

"Sam, put him out."

The Toff half-turned. As he did so, he caught a glimpse of a small shrivelled-looking man who was already raising his right arm; in the hand was a cosh, a lead-weighted implement reckoned to induce unconsciousness without doing permanent injury.

The Toff turned fully, and let go a pile-driver to the shrivelled man's stomach. He drove it home, and the cosh dropped from a nerveless hand. In the Toff's mind there was a hope that he could grab the little fellow and use him as a cover against the gun, but he reckoned without the gunman's speed of movement. He had gripped a thin waist when he

37

saw the gun upraised and butt foremost.

The girl screamed.

The butt descended, and the Toff felt the blow on the side of the head. The pain was sharp, and he slipped, tried to get up, then felt a second and more vicious blow on the temple. He had just time to be aware of the pain, an unbearable one; then he lost consciousness.

He did not see the gunman grip Iris's wrists, nor hear him swear at her, nor see a third man come from the trees with a scarf in his hands. He did not see the scarf wound tightly about the girl's mouth, so that she could not talk or cry for help, nor see the quartette – after the shrivelled little man had recovered – start for a road running across the gorse-land, and hidden from the cottage by the trees.

Nor did he feel the shrivelled man's boot, when the man turned back and kicked him in the ribs.

"Stop that," called the man with the pale face, and reluctantly Sam turned. The girl was forced to hurry, with a hand gripping her arm painfully. They reached the road, and a car standing by it, the girl was bundled in, and Sam took the wheel. The few people who saw them did not notice anything unusual about the car or its occupants.

*

The first thing the Toff knew about returning consciousness was pain in his head. It was so acute that he gritted his teeth, a grinding pressure that throbbed and ached, and did not ease when he tried to open his eyes.

He was on his side, and his legs were drawn up.

He straightened them slowly, and found it easier when he laid his head on the soft, springy turf. He stayed like that for an immeasurable time until he was able to open his eyes with less difficulty. The trees kept the slanting rays of the sun from him, for which he was grateful.

Very slowly, he sat up.

That was not too good, for his head swam, and the pain was renewed. But he forced himself to stand, swaying from side to side and stretching out to grip a bush close to him. Thus steadied, he felt easier, and with difficulty he took out his cigarette-case and lit a cigarette. Although his mouth was dry he felt an imperative need to smoke.

His mind began to function.

The girl – the man with the pale face – Sam, who was like a shrivelled monkey. The silence of the other's approach was explained by the springy turf. Rollison attempted, very slowly, to walk. In five minutes he had discovered a little hiding-place. It was littered with cigarette ends, and he picked some of them up, tossed them away when he saw that they were all of the same popular brand. There was not enough of them left to hold finger-prints, and millions of men smoked the same kind.

Then he put a hand to his head. His fingers were covered with blood when he drew them away. He grimaced, shrugged, and walked towards the cottage.

He had no idea how long he had been unconscious, for his watch had broken in his fall – or what he thought had been his fall – until he grew aware of a painful ache in his left side. The ache increased with every step, and then he saw a bruise on his wrist, near the watch.

There were no stones against which he could have fallen.

He realized that he had been kicked, and did not think it likely that events would prove him wrong.

The cottage seemed, to his painful progress, a mile off. Three cars remained outside it – his own, the doctor's, and presumably a police car. He was nearing them when some-one shouted from one side of the cart-track.

"Hi, you!"

He half-turned, and saw a constable hurrying towards him. The man's face was red and wet with perspiration, and he gave the impression of being angry.

"Where've *you* been! I – here, are you all right?"

He had seen the lacerated patch on the Toff's temple, and his anger evaporated.

He had, he said, been looking everywhere for him.

"How did you know my name?"

"I see you batting," said the constable, as if that explained everything.

A clock in the room where Defoe had been found showed that it was nearly quarter to nine. He had not been unconscious for more than ten or fifteen minutes, Rollison reasoned; perhaps altogether half an hour had passed from the time he had been knocked out to the moment when the constable had called him.

In the room was Whittaker, and a tall, lean-faced, middle-aged man with sharp grey eyes.

"I found him, sir," said the constable triumphantly.

Rollison looked vaguely at the lean-faced man, while Whittaker stepped forward quickly.

"Sit down, Mr. Rollison. Constable, get me some of that hot water, will you?" Rollison sat down, and felt at once very tired and very comfortable. Once or twice Whittaker hurt him, but when he had finished bathing and dressing the wound it was surprisingly comfortable.

"All I really need now is a cup of tea," he said. "I'll feel a new man then."

"Simm can make one," said Whittaker. He went out of the room, leaving Rollison alone with the lean-faced man. The constable hovered by the door until the senior officer told him to stay in the garden.

Rollison regarded his companion half-humorously.

"Should we know each other?"

"I'm Inspector Bright, of the Surrey C.I.D.," said the other promptly. "I've had your name." He did not look pleased to know Rollison. "To save time, I think I should tell you that I have heard of you, also."

"Well, that's something."

"I shall want a full statement very quickly," said Bright.

"I don't blame you. But you'll be wise to wait for an hour or two – anything I say now would be a bit vague, for I'd forget so much. Could you see me at the Hall –"

"Mr. Rollison, I want to make myself quite clear," said Bright crisply. "You have been known to keep facts of importance from the authorities, and you might be said to have a certain kind of reputation. I want you to understand that this matter must be handled by the police, and in accordance with police regulations. I am not prepared to accede to you any special indulgence because –" He paused.

"Go on," said Rollison gently.

"You know quite well what I mean."

"Yes. Because on occasions Scotland Yard has indulged me," said Rollison. "You know your business, Inspector, but I'm not happy about your manner. What makes you think that I might try to take advantage of – my reputation?"

"You were seen on the road with a young woman. Who was she?"

"Young woman," said the Toff, and pressed his fingers lightly against his bandaged head. "Yes. She did tell me her name, but I've forgotten it." He lied quite easily, for he was not then prepared to make any statement to Bright, and he had good reason for pretending that he could not make a comprehensive one.

Bright drew a sharp breath; doubtless he suspected that the lapse of memory was intentional; as certainly he knew

41

that he could not reasonably do anything about it. When Whittaker came in again, with some tea, Bright went to the window and looked out.

"How do you feel?" asked Whittaker.

"Almost light-headed," said the Toff. "An hour's sleep would do me a world of good."

"Yes, yes." Rollison did not know whether he was imagining things, but he fancied that he saw a glint of humour in the doctor's bright blue eyes. "I think you should get back to the Hall – I'll take you. Most unwise for you to attempt to drive yourself."

"I'm quite sure I don't feel up to it," said Rollison.

"I can see no reason why you shouldn't make a statement now," said Bright sharply.

Whittaker looked about to protest, but the Toff spoke before him.

"I'll make one, if you want it." He sounded very weary. "I'm confused over details of what happened before I was knocked out, but I was with this girl – what the devil *is* her name? – when three not very prepossessing men arrived. I had the impression that they had been watching the cottage. I was slugged over the head – one of the trio showed a gun, by the way, and I couldn't do much – and I woke up and came straight here."

"Where did you meet the girl?"

Rollison pressed his temple again, very lightly.

"She was walking near the cottage."

"You know, Inspector, I think you'll be wise to leave this for an hour or two," said Whittaker. "Mr. Rollison should be much clearer-headed then. At the moment he will only confuse himself by trying to recall incidents."

"I can tell you one thing," said the Toff. "She said she'd been to the cottage and seen Defoe – she was an acquaintance of his. He was hurt when she arrived, but I don't

42

know what time it was. The three thugs didn't give me much chance for talking."

Bright was ungracious – not without cause.

"If you go to the Hall, I shall want to send one of my men with you. Please give him a statement as soon as you are able." He sneered the last words, and then went out of the room.

Whittaker regarded the Toff silently, and there was no longer any doubt that he was amused.

"A very zealous officer," he said. "But I presume you need a little time to put your thoughts into some kind of order, Mr. Rollison. Let's get out to the car –"

"It wouldn't be a bad idea if Bright's man drove mine after us," said Rollison. "Will you put it to him?"

Whittaker chuckled.

"Yes, I will." He went out ahead of the Toff, who was wondering why the doctor should be so helpful, and how much it would be wise to leave out of his statement. It was the fear in the girl's eyes, so vividly remembered, that persuaded him to hold his peace until he had his thoughts in better order, and he concentrated on arranging them as Whittaker drove him to the Hall, and the policeman drove the Frazer Nash behind them.

Behind the Frazer Nash followed a small Austin, with a man at the wheel whom the Toff had not seen, but who had bound Iris Brent's mouth with a scarf.

CHAPTER SIX

Questions of Importance

WHITTAKER did little talking on the journey to the Hall. It was past ten o'clock when the arrived. The dusk had deepened to a near-darkness, and there was only the after-glow in the western sky. The little Austin had driven past the imposing wrought-iron gates of the big house when the policeman had turned the Frazer Nash in the wake of Whittaker's car.

The Toff had seen the small car, but had given it little attention. For one thing, he was feeling the effects of the blow more than he had done at the cottage, and the ache in his side was not getting easier. He found it impossible to concentrate as he wanted. Matters of importance grew confused with those of little consequence, but through the mists which gathered in his mind there emerged one major question.

What should he do about Iris Brent?

He had seen her expression when the gunman had arrived, and did not think the fear he had seen there was because of the gun; she had recognized Pale Face; and the latter's words had given the impression that he also knew her.

Apparently the crook's main purpose had been to kidnap her. They had not done much harm to him; had simply put him out so that he could do nothing to help the girl – to whom he had promised help, but failed so signally to assist.

That was not a pleasant thought.

He tried to put it out of his mind as they drew up outside the Hall, a large Georgian building, well-kept and well-preserved, with the walls half hidden with ivy and clematis. Green shutters were at all the windows, the porch was imposing, supported by four stone pillars and approached by a short flight of stone steps. The massive front door was painted green, like the shutters, and the knocker and letter-box were of brass, polished so that they shone even in that dull light.

"How are you feeling?" Whittaker asked as he climbed out.

"Worse than I thought likely."

"I'm not surprised," Whittaker was brisk. "I think you are liable to over-estimate your strength, Mr. Rollison. Er – I gather that Bright was a little afraid that you would throw your weight about – if I may put it like that." The portly doctor was diffident.

"So you've heard of my habits, too?"

"Oh yes. I didn't associate you with the – er – Toff when I saw you batting this afternoon. A fine knock – I haven't seen a better since Defoe scored a hundred and five in fifty minutes, earlier in the season. But you won't want to chatter about that now. If you take my advice you'll go to your room and lie down for at least a couple of hours, without a light. Don't eat anything solid – broth, or bread-and-milk."

"Oh, Great Scott!" exclaimed the Toff. "Not invalid diet yet!" He staggered a little as he climbed out, and Whittaker raised an arm to support him. "Perhaps you're right," he added glumly. "But just now I don't want to be out of action. In fact –"

The policeman had left his car and was approaching. Rollison stopped speaking and went to the front door. His head was surprisingly dizzy, his side ached abominably.

"It must have been a hefty clout," he said. "Come up with me, will you, and have a look at my side. Something's wrong with that, too. And fend off Mary and Bill Crossfield, if you can."

Whittaker was as capable at the Hall as he had been at the cottage. In less than ten minutes Rollison was lying on his bed, with his shoes off and his collar and tie loosened. Bill Crossfield had not yet returned from London, and Mary, although anxious took the doctor's word that the guest should not be disturbed for some time. The policeman parked himself outside the Toff's door, and there was little doubt that the law's presence sent a wave of gossip through the servant's quarters.

45

Most of this Whittaker told him as he examined the bruises in his side. And:

"A good rub with embrocation will do them good," he said, "but you'll be stiff for a few days. Can I help you in any other way?"

Rollison said:

"Yes, if you will. I'd like my man to start looking for a girl named Brent, Iris Brent. Will you telephone my flat – Mayfair 02133 – and ask him to get busy? He goes by the name of Jolly."

"Isn't it rather a tall order?" asked Whittaker.

"Jolly's used to tall orders," said the Toff. "It will be enough for him to start on. I suppose the name doesn't mean anything to you? Iris Brent . . ."

"No." Whittaker did not try to hide his curiosity. "Is that the girl who was seen with you?"

"Yes. And confidentially, I can't make up my mind whether to tell the police about her or not. I –" He broke off and grimaced. "Leave it with me for an hour or two, will you? And if you're not too tired, and should come along to see your patient about twelve o'clock, I might be very talkative. There's a lot to be talked about."

"All right." Whittaker was crisp. "Try not to worry too much, Mr. Rollison, give yourself a chance to get over the bang on the head."

He left Rollison still worried and concerned. Was he being wise not to mention the girl? Was she in acute danger? What mattered most to her – being freed, or keeping her presence – or rather her identity – from the police? The question resolved itself into one which he could not answer. Had the fear in her eyes been there because she was afraid the police would know that she had been at the cottage, or was it concerned with something else – with Pale Face, for instance?

46

He said aloud: "Oh, well, I'll take the chance that she's more worried about the police than Pale Face.' '

It was a decision of sorts, and after making it he dozed for half an hour, then fell into a deep sleep. Afterwards he said that it was the least auspicious beginning to any case in which he had been interested, because it was twelve hours after he was introduced to it before he could think to any purpose. Those twelve hours might have proved fatal; they did not, but he often said that it was not his fault that things worked better for Iris Brent than they might have done.

*

In his youth they had called the man 'Pasty'.

Since he had been born and bred in the East End of London, amid the squalor of dockside cottages and the lusty coarseness of stevedores and dock-labourers, Lascars and Dutchmen, Chinese and Maltese, men of all nations, all creeds, all degrees of morality and immorality, it was surprising that the nickname was not coarser.

He had no real name.

For the first nine years of his life he knew little of kindness, for the woman who 'cared' for him was a slatternly lodging-house keeper who did so because she received two pound notes each month by registered letter. She did not know who sent them; she knew only that the child had been literally left on her doorstep, with a five-pound note pinned to its shawl, and a promise of more if she looked after him.

Even as a child the remarkable pallor had been in evidence, so that he had looked a puling infant, not long to stand the rigours of the upbringing he was likely to have. But the pallor was a deceptive thing. Organically he was strong, and he had no serious illness, gave Ma Parker little trouble, and soon after he could toddle fetched her fish-and-chips from a shop in the Mile End Road. Later, when his balance was more reliable, he was entrusted with the nightly task of bringing her a pint of porter in a cracked earthenware jug from the pub on the corner of Gay Street.

What sardonic humorist had called it Gay Street no one in the vicinity knew. It was dirty, and the houses were no more than hovels. There were no front gardens, for the front doors opened on to the pavement, and there were little patches of black earth at the back.

Railway arches stood near by, tall sentinels watching over Gay Street's cosmopolitan fraternity.

What kindness went Pasty's way was in rough words and coarse jests from men who noticed him, who ruffled his black hair, and occasionally told him stories of the great high seas. Thus into his half-formed mind there was placed a determination to go to sea, to get away from the squalor of Gay Street. Even then, he showed a remarkable fastidiousness, and was sometimes found washing furtively, and brushing his teeth with a toothbrush bought with the few coppers which came his way.

The Mongol touch in him bespoke a mixed parentage. None knew who the parents were. But there were times when he showed a streak of callousness undoubtedly inherited from the East. He had something of the Orient's inscrutability, and much of its ability to endure pain. Beatings he took without apparent resentment, growing hardened to them, sometimes deliberately inviting one by doing what he should not in plain sight of Ma Parker or one of her cronies.

Just before his tenth birthday he attracted attention in the school he attended three streets away. A middle-aged bachelor teacher found his mind surprisingly sharp, even amongst the sharp-witted Cockneys; so Pasty went from time to time to the teacher's two humble rooms in Bethnal Green, and showed an avidness in learning that swiftly took

48

him beyond the school's curriculum. He won a scholarship at the age of eleven, and went to a secondary school, still staying with Ma Parker. He was a prodigy at the second school, also; and when the opportunity came for him to go to Oxford he took it after a fierce argument with Ma Parker, who was afraid that if he did so her allowance, which came with such mysterious frequency, would stop.

It did.

At Oxford, Pasty, who went also by the name of Herbert Lossen, after an adult boarder of Ma Parker's, concealed the cruel streak latent in him and earned considerable fame. He had a fierce manner, and a sharp tongue which often took him into trouble, but in the debating society he was an opponent to be feared – except that he had none of the usual convictions, and did not take a great interest in politics as such. He spoke on Social Reform; it was his one subject. But after a while his interest in that faded, and at twenty-one, with a first-class education behind him, but no background, he applied for and obtained a position in the Crossfield Shipping Company.

He knew little about the Crossfields.

He did know that at the time Julian Crossfield – father of Mary and Bill – controlled the destiny of the Manufacturing Company, the Shipping Company, the Colliery Company, the Iron and Steel Company – every company, in fact, which was in the great Crossfield Combine. After a year he applied for and obtained the post of New York manager for the Shipping Company. It was there that he first met men who positively benefited from breaking the law, and in nineteen-thirty he was one of several Big Shots who were arrested and charged in one of the periodical clean-ups of the rum- and gun-runners of New York State.

A clever attorney cleared him; an uncompromising Julian Crossfield cabled immediately afterwards to say that he was

49

removed from his position, and was being immediately replaced. Crossfield prevented any legal action by sending him one year's salary, and Herbert Lossen, still called Pasty, then turned with a deepening interest to the affairs of the New York underworld. In time he found things too hot for him, and with a comparatively comfortable fortune returned to England.

In the meantime Julian Crossfield had died, and Arnold had replaced him as head of the companies. Bill Crossfield, who had no inclination to work, had been left the bulk of his father's fortune in trust until he was twenty-seven. Arnold held the purse-strings, as the Toff had discovered, and had insisted on Bill taking a more active interest in the companies which bore his name.

In England, Lossen found the habit of law-keeping strange and unwelcome. Then he was visited at his London hotel by a man who had known of his New York activities, and put to him a proposition which was particularly interesting. Lossen accepted the proposition the more eagerly because it was made by a man who found the Crossfield Companies too competitive, and wanted them restricted. Lossen considered that the Crossfields had cheated him; the opportunity to take revenge could not be missed. All these factors had weighed in the mind of the man who had approached him.

None of them, of course, was suspected by the Toff.

He knew Herbert Lossen as Pale Face and he knew that Pale Face had taken the girl away. He did not know that as he slept at Crossfield Hall she was taken to a small house on the outskirts of Staines, put into an attic room, and left there, still gagged tightly enough to prevent her from trying to attract attention. Lossen visited her just after midnight.

"Keep quiet, and cause no trouble," he told her, "and you'll be all right. If you're awkward –" He paused, and did not make his meaning clear by words, yet he contrived to make her feel very frightened.

Then he asked her what she knew of Rollison: she told him, and Lossen – who had spent little time in the East End since his return to England, and knew only vaguely of the Toff – thought of Rollison as an interfering amateur who could be easily dealt with if he proved troublesome. He was, in any case, being watched.

Lossen closed and locked the door on Iris Brent: and thirty miles away Dr. Whittaker entered Rollison's room as the patient stirred and opened his eyes.

CHAPTER SEVEN

More of Defoe

SLEEP had performed a miracle.

Rollison awakened clear-headed and, apart from stiffness in his head and at his side, very near to normal. Whittaker felt his pulse, took his temperature, and put his head on one side.

"I think I was wrong," he said. "You can't over-estimate your strength! I haven't known a recovery as quick and complete as yours seems to be."

"Good," said Rollison. "And what about food?"

"We-ell – a few sandwiches. Don't overdo it. And you're not going to try to go out tonight, are you?"

"I don't know," said Rollison. He rang a bell, and sent a maid for sandwiches. When the door closed: "Did you get Jolly?"

"Yes."

"Thanks. Has Bright been worrying you?"

"No."

51

"Better. How is Defoe?"

Whittaker frowned.

"He's got something in common with you, Mr. Rollison – a surprising power of recovery. I think nine men out of ten would have been on the danger list for a week or more after what Defoe suffered, but he's comfortable. There'll be no need for an operation, although he's had a blood-transfusion. He won't die – I suppose that's what you want to know?"

"It's the first thing," said Rollison. "What do you know about him?"

Whittaker pursed his lips.

"Very little – and I shan't be betraying any confidences if I tell you. He's been living at the cottage on and off for three years. He rents it from the estate, of course."

"Why 'of course'?"

"Everything about here belongs to the Crossfields," said Whittaker. "But there's rather more in it than there appears on the surface. Sir Julian – you know the history of the family, I assume?"

"The recent history, yes." Rollison was sitting in an easy chair, and smoking. "Sir Julian built up the business – should I say businesses? – and bought this estate fifty years ago. His brother now controls the commercial activities and the estate is run by a manager. Lady Crossfield is a pleasant woman who doesn't carry much weight. Mary's a live wire, and Bill's lazy."

Whittaker's eyes crinkled at the corners.

"That's a fair estimate," he admitted. "And you didn't waste a word! Well, then – both Julian and Arnold Crossfield were very strict. Defoe's hardly the type of tenant you would expect them to have for more than one year."

"I gather that he's a ladies' man," said Rollison dryly.

"There isn't much doubt of that," said Whittaker. "Mind you, I like the fellow. I always have done. I shouldn't talk

52

about him but for the fact that I think you – er – you're likely to be very active. What I say is in strict confidence, of course."

"Of course."

"Thank you. He does have lady guests at the cottage, and very frequently. His – er – taste is excellent." Whittaker smiled, a little awkwardly, as if the attitude of a man-of-the-world did not really suit him. "As far as I know he's single, but his frequent lady visitors have caused a great deal of talk in the village, particularly since Crossfield has allowed him to continue there."

"But surely if he had an agreement –"

"For one year only," said Whittaker. "It's surprising what we know about each other in Fern Cross, Mr. Rollison! Actually, Defoe made it well known when he came here that he was trying the cottage out for a year, and would stay longer only if it suited him. The village was quite certain that he wouldn't suit the Crossfields. Instead, he's still there."

"I should imagine he was a good tenant."

"An excellent one, but –" Whittaker stood up and began to pace the room. "It's not really easy to let you see the atmosphere of Fern Cross, and the Crossfields. Sir Julian was an eccentric, and very nearly a dictator. He looked after the village very well – all the villages and all the farms, for that matter. There are never any complaints about the state of the cottages in the district, and repairs are done promptly as they become necessary. Arnold continues to have the same thought for the tenants, through the estate manager – the same one, of course, whom Sir Julian employed. But if there is any scandal or gossip, and good grounds for it – then a tenant goes at the end of his first agreement. It's something almost feudal – you do see what I'm driving at, don't you?"

53

"Yes," said Rollison slowly. "Quite well. So there's a mystery about Defoe, who shouldn't have been allowed to stay. The suggestion is, of course, that he has some pull with Arnold Crossfield."

"I have heard it said openly, yes."

"Does he ever visit the Hall?"

"He's never been known to. Er – you'll probably find that Mary and Bill, and Lady Crossfield for that matter, know nothing about the talk in the village. They're very popular, and I don't think any villager would cause them any trouble."

"Yes, that fits," admitted Rollison. "The whole world can be talking about a man's wife, but the husband doesn't hear a word of it. It's odd, to say the least. You're sure you haven't heard of this girl – Iris Brent?"

"I'm quite sure. She may have been one of Defoe's friends, of course. You found her at the cottage, didn't you?"

Rollison smiled.

"If I tell you anything more about her you'll be in bad with Bright, and that wouldn't do. But if you care to be on hand while I give Bright's policeman a stateman, you'll read a lot between the lines. Unless the policeman objects –"

"Oh, Featherby won't mind me," said Whittaker.

Police-Constable Featherby, a middle-aged man who could write shorthand, did not mind Dr. Whittaker. He took down Rollison's statement quickly. Rollison related the arrival at the cottage, the finding of Defoe, the start for a doctor – picking up the girl on the way, he said – the meeting with the doctor, and the examination of the ground outside the cottage. He said more: that the girl had told him she was on the way to see Defoe, and that he had advised her not to go to the cottage. She had given him her name, and asked him to tell her how Defoe progressed, but he could not remember her address. Her name, he thought, was Gent. He couldn't be sure, because just as she had told him the three men had appeared, and he had been knocked out.

When P.C. Featherby had gone, Whittaker rubbed his ample chin.

"Yes, I can read between the lines, Mr. Rollison! Bright will be able to, also."

"I think I can make Bright happier as time goes on," said Rollison. "I'll have a good try, anyhow."

Whittaker shrugged.

"You know your own business best. Well, it's late and I must be going. Er – you're sure it's wise to leave the girl's name out, I suppose? Presumably since when you were attacked she was – er – persuaded to go with your attackers. It might be wiser if the police were able to look for her."

Rollison said: "I'm not taking anything for granted Doctor. And thanks a lot for your help."

"Oh, that's all right. And if I can help again I'll be delighted. Delighted," repeated Whittaker, shook hands, and went out.

It was three-quarters of an hour later, when the Toff had decided that there was nothing he could usefully do until the morning, that the extension telephone in his bedroom rang. He lifted the receiver, and a deep, somewhat sonorous voice answered him.

"Mr. Rollison, please."

"Speaking, Jolly," said Rollison.

"Good evening, sir," said Jolly, without regard to the fact that it was between 1 and 2 a.m. "I duly received your message, and made inquiries along the lines which I imagined you would desire –"

"At this time of morning, let's have less verbosity," said the Toff.

"Very good, sir. The lady in question *could* be one in

55

whom there has been considerable public interest recently, sir."

"Where?"

"In some sections of the Press," said Jolly carefully. "Shall I read the articles out to you over the telephone?"

"Is there anything that might be urgent?"

"I am hardly in a position to make a statement to that effect, sir. The articles are all a week old – perhaps you would prefer me to come down at once, sir, and bring the information with me."

"On the whole I think that'll be best," said Rollison. "It will take you an hour and a half – leave at half past five, Jolly, then there'll be someone up and about when you arrive. Tell them to call me immediately, and you come straight up to my room."

"Very good, sir," said Jolly.

He rang down, and the Toff replaced the telephone slowly. He was not wholly surprised, but he was pleased. The anxiety which the girl had shown to keep her name from the police suggested the possibility that her chief fear was of publicity; it looked as if she had had a share of it within the past week. There would be much to help him in Jolly's press-cuttings, and the few hours which would elapse would surely make little or no difference.

He was uneasy, nevertheless, when he undressed and at last went properly to bed.

The sun was shining through a top corner of his window when he was awakened by a sharp tap at the door. He struggled to a sitting position, winced when he twisted his side, and then he saw Jolly entering.

A man of medium height and rather scraggy, his expression one of dignified melancholy, Jolly's face was lined, and at the mouth drooped as a bloodhound's lips droop, or at least in a passable imitation. The Toff had often told him that he would make an excellent musical-comedy butler, to which Jolly invariably replied that he hoped he gave satisfaction where he was.

Jolly, despite his dyspeptic countenance, was a man of surprises, and sharp-witted withal. The Toff knew of no one on whom he could depend more thoroughly.

That morning Jolly had clearly been exerting a persuasive charm, for he carried with him a tea-tray, and biscuits. He looked sharply at the Toff's bandaged head, and put the tray on a pedestal cupboard.

"Would you have preferred coffee, sir?"

"No, tea will do fine," said Rollison. "I'm sorry to interrupt your holiday, Jolly."

"I was finding it heavy on my hands, sir," declared Jolly. "If I may say so, I am never so fully occupied when I am in London on my own, and I was looking forward to your return." He poured out tea; on the tray were two cups.

"And one for yourself," said Rollison, to whom the two cups was a hint not to be ignored. "Where are those cuttings?"

"I will get them, sir." Jolly took a large envelope from his inside coat pocket, opened it, took out a dozen or more press cuttings, some of them with headlines, and not until they were in a position where the Toff could read them comfortably did he pour out a second cup of tea. "Thank you, sir. The journey gave me no time for refreshment."

As he drank, he watched his employer.

As Rollison sipped, he scanned the cuttings.

They concerned Iris Brent; of that there was no doubt at all, for on four cuttings there was her photograph, although poor likenesses even for newspaper reproduction, but the width of her forehead, the shortness of her nose and the attractiveness of the whole could hardly be mistaken. That established in his mind, he read the first article.

CHAPTER EIGHT

And More of Iris

THE thing which surprised the Toff most was that he had seen nothing of the articles on the previous Friday, when they had appeared. Normally he scanned most of the daily papers, for often he found in them an item of interest and occasionally a paragraph which so intrigued him that he made inquiries about it; thus some of the most outstanding cases in his career had started.

Then he recalled that on the previous Thursday he had been with a small party which had gone from place to place in the amusement called a treasure hunt. It had lasted until the early hours; it had bored him, and it had made him sleep late. When he had awakened a friend had been waiting to see him, and he had left Gresham Terrace not only without reading the papers but also without anything substantial in the way of breakfast. Spending the evening and the night in the country, the evening papers had not come his way.

And, as was the habit of newspaper sensations, a headline one day was worthy only of a paragraph the next.

So he had missed the story of Iris Brent, which was brief enough in all conscience, for each of the articles said the same thing; she had been interviewed by many reporters, but had given remarkably little away.

The most typical headline read:

GIRL WITHRAWS BREACH CASE

That was another surprising item; it was absurd to try to form a judgment on a short acquaintance, yet he often did so, and was nearly as often right. He would not have thought that Iris Brent would take her romance, broken or otherwise, into court, and thus the public eye. Apparently she had regretted her first decision, and although the case had been down for hearing that week, she had withdrawn it. There were comments from a judge, who apparently thought she should have made up her mind well before she did, and there was a statement that Miss Brent was a private secretary – her employer's name was not mentioned – that she was twenty-four, and that she had been engaged to Mr. Patrick Defoe for two years.

The name of Defoe did not surprise him.

In fact it explained something of the reason for her visit, more of her reason for wanting to be kept out of the lime-light of publicity. Defoe attacked – his ex-fiancée near the scene of the crime; few people would have failed to judge her before she was tried.

The Toff looked up from the articles, after making sure that there was no mention of her employer in any cutting.

"Whom did she work for, Jolly?"

"I made inquiries about that subject, sir, particularly with a view to discovering why the gentleman's name had been suppressed. I found none, sir – but I was able to as-certain that for some six months she has been employed as private secretary to Mr. Arnold Crossfield."

Jolly made that statement without batting an eye.

Rollison's stare grew more intent, and for some seconds the room was very silent. Then he pushed the bed-clothes to one side.

"Run me a bath, Jolly – the room's next door but one."

"Very good, sir. Are you sure your head is all right for such exertion?"

"I'm going to try it," said the Toff.

A warm bath did much to ease the aching in his side; after

it he secured some embrocation from Bill Crossfield, who had returned at midnight and gone straight to bed, so that Jolly could rub it in. The bruises were badly coloured, purple, red and black mingling; whoever had kicked him had certainly been vicious.

While he had bathed, Jolly had breakfasted, and also arranged for Rollison to breakfast in his room. It was served as soon as Rollison was dressed, and while he ate bacon and kidneys with tomatoes and mushrooms – with keen enjoyment – for his abstinence of the previous evening made him exceptionally hungry – he gave Jolly a *résumé* of the affair as far as he knew it. Jolly made no comments, but carefully assimilated every detail. The narrative was finished with a final cup of coffee. Then:

"Well, Jolly, what do you make of it?"

"It is somewhat confused, sir, and a little early to attempt to come to any conclusion."

"Yes." Rollison lit a cigarette and strolled to the window. "It's one of the most curious mix-ups I've ever come across. She works for Arnold Crossfield, and is engaged to Defoe, who lives at the Crossfield Estate and does not have the reputation which most good tenants should have. Nothing is done about that, however, and the village is very gossip-ridden. One might say scandalized."

"Would it be advisable, sir, for me to try to find what I can in the village? I have little doubt that I shall find them discursive, now that Mr. Defoe has been hurt."

"An excellent idea. Consider it to be your job, for the time being. Mine is – well, what is mine, Jolly?"

"Finding Miss Brent, sir?"

"Ye-es. A primary task, of course, but not an easy one. I wonder if we've a theory that will fit the facts? She puts up this breach case. Defoe, a fascinating individual by all

60

accounts, persuades her to withdraw it, and asks her to see him today."

"Yesterday, sir," corrected Jolly.

"We know what I mean. She arrives and finds him badly hurt. She sees these three men, who go away after spending most of the day at the cottage. The assumption is that they searched it comprehensively, and had time to put everything back in good order before the police arrived."

"That is so, sir."

"Then what? They go, and she returns. What's the point I haven't mentioned, Jolly?"

"One peculiar fact emerges, sir. If the three men attacked Defoe in the first place, as she appears to imagine, they had no intention of killing him – otherwise they would have made sure, for they certainly had ample opportunity."

"So we see that the same way," said Rollison slowly. "Why didn't they finish their job?"

"The assumption that they started it isn't borne out, sir."

"No, it isn't," said Rollison. He returned sharply from the window. "The three men would have finished him off if they'd started the job. So presumably someone other than the trio knifed him."

"And the trio's arrival drove the someone away, sir?"

"No. Miss Brent's did. *If* she's telling the truth," added Rollison, "and I hope that she is, Jolly, I hope so very much indeed."

"I gathered that you were well impressed by the young lady, sir."

"Don't gather too much," said the Toff absently. "There's another queer thing. Someone thought it necessary to do some gardening. I wonder if the police have reached that point yet."

61

"If they didn't see it yesterday, sir, they will have no opportunity now."

"No. All right, Jolly. Go downstairs, and try to find what you can about Defoe. As always, anything will be worth picking up – trivialities as well as major facts. And, Jolly –"

"Yes, sir?"

"Find the popular opinion on Mr. Arnold Crossfield."

When Jolly had gone, the Toff put the cuttings in his suit-case, locked it, and then went downstairs. He met Bill Crossfield coming from the breakfast-room. Bill was concerned, and showed a tendency to feel that Rollison should be treated as an invalid. Rollison discouraged it, and:

"Did you get on all right yesterday, Bill?"

Crossfield scowled.

"Oh, I suppose so. Why the devil he sent for me I don't know – it was some pesty meeting, and he didn't call it until the morning. He knew I was spending a week-end down here."

Rollison smiled.

"His idea of a week-end and yours don't tally. But if it wasn't important, it was too bad."

Crossfield grinned.

"Not for you – I gather you had a good time for an hour or two! You're a sly devil – why didn't you tell me you were a cricketer. You came down here for tennis, didn't you?"

"I'm committing the cardinal crime of mixing the games," said Rollison.

"You mean Mary persuaded you to give up cricket for the week-end," said Bill Crossfield, and in fact that was partly true, for the invitation had come from Mary, who knew Rollison reasonably well. He had been attracted by the thought of a quiet week-end with tennis the main re-creation. He had, in fact, been prepared to be lazy.

He sometimes thought, when he felt like that, that he was

getting old; was one old at thirty-two?

That thought did not persist, and Crossfield frowned again.

"It's a bad show about Defoe, isn't it? That's where you got your bang, I'm told?" Obviously he did not know much of what had happened, and the Toff told him as much as he felt was wise. While they were talking, Mary came in, her cheeks glowing from a ride through the parkland. She was wearing a yellow blouse, open at the neck, jodhpurs and stout shoes. Her hair was a little untidy, her blue eyes shining.

They narrowed at sight of Rollison.

"Rolly, ought you to be up?"

"For once and for all, I refute the suggestion that I am still convalescing," said Rollison. "It's not half as bad as this bandage makes it look."

"I don't believe you," said Mary flatly, and took his arm. "Is there any coffee left, Bill?"

"I think so." Crossfield went upstairs, as Mary and Rollison went in to breakfast. Slowly, Mary said:

"Isn't it a beast of a business? I had to go for a gallop to get it out of my mind."

"Why worry about it at all?" asked Rollison.

"Oh, don't be ridiculous!" She spoke sharply, and he fancied that she coloured a little. "Everyone liked Defoe, and it's a miserable thing to have happened."

"I see," said Rollison, and reflected that by 'everyone' Mary probably meant herself and Bill. Had Defoe's fascination attracted her, too? He did not think that she would readily talk, but he was wrong in part. She told him she knew about the breach-of-promise case, that she had seen the girl's photograph, and:

"Do you think she had anything to do with it?"

63

"I haven't had time to think," said Rollison. "Why should I pick on her, anyhow?"

"I thought perhaps you would agree with the police."

Rollison covered his surprise.

"In what?"

"You *are* ill," declared Mary. "Or else that reputation of yours is all hooey. I thought you knew everything, and worked hand in hand with the police."

"You're wrong on both counts," said Rollison. "Tell me more about it – unless you're talking for the sake of talking."

"Well, I'm not. I met Featherby in the village, and he told me that they're looking for the girl – Iris Brent, isn't it?"

The Toff thought a little ruefully that he need not have kept the story back from the police after all. Then he changed his mind; they did not know the girl had been near the cottage, and by talking he would have made the appearances against her look even worse.

Moreover, he was relieved.

He was still more relieved an hour later when he was sitting in the small office allocated to Inspector Bright, in Guildford. Bright was cheerful that morning – Rollison suspected that he had been in touch with Scotland Yard; there were times when the Yard encouraged Rollison, for it was a fact that he often obtained results when they had failed.

"I'm glad you've come," said Bright, and pulled a typewritten statement towards him on a desk littered with papers. "Do you mind reading this statement through and signing it?"

The Toff took the statement.

"Provided your man hasn't added any touches, I'll sign it gladly." As he read, Bright watched him, and when he took a fountain-pen from his pocket the policeman said quickly:

"You still don't remember the girl's name?"

"No."

"You've said there that you think it was 'Gent'."

"Something like that, yes."

"What about Brent?"

"Well, it rhymes," smiled the Toff, "but I couldn't guarantee anything. Brent, Brent – great Scott, I remember! No, not her name," he added quickly, and an expression of satisfaction disappeared from Bright's face. "The breach case, wasn't it? And Defoe – damn it, surely Defoe was the defendant, or would have been had the case matured?"

Bright looked disappointed.

"So you know about that?"

"I remember it," admitted Rollison suavely. He scribbled his signature and added: "I remember thinking that it was queer that her employer's name wasn't mentioned. Usually the Press brings in what names it can when there's no chance of libel."

Bright did not rise to the bait.

"Wasn't it mentioned? I suppose it's not important. Well, if you remember nothing else, that's all you can do for me." He pulled the statement towards him. "I have a feeling that it's going to be very simple, Mr. Rollison. It shouldn't be difficult to identify the woman you met on the road. In fact, she's been identified up to a point, but I'm hoping to take the identification a stage further." Quite quickly, and with the air of a conjurer, he brought a large photograph from beneath the papers on his desk, and held it towards the Toff, so that the latter looked on the set face of Iris Brent again. "Was that the girl?"

Rollison hesitated.

"Oh, come," said Bright, who was certainly no fool, and

had clearly carefully rehearsed this. "The three men who saw you with her in your car have already said it was her. You can't be in doubt – it was a clear evening, and this is an excellent photograph. Was that the girl?"

Rollison said carefully:

"I wouldn't be prepared to swear to it, from that photograph, any more than the three cricketers who identified it 'up to a point' would. There's a likeness, yes. But I was in a hurry, and anxious to get the doctor. I didn't spend time examining her features. Have you found her?"

"Yes," said Inspector Bright calmly, and he sat back as if to enjoy that triumph.

CHAPTER NINE

A Question of Identity

THE Toff had no reason to doubt the statement.

He was a little perturbed, for it was likely that the police would obtain a full statement from the girl, and unlikely that she would confirm his story of what had happened on the previous evening. But there was nothing he could do about that, and he felt a sense of anticlimax. The fuss and the bother, especially the wound in the head, had not been worth it.

That, he afterwards admitted, was when he was almost dejected. There were many things in the Crossfield affair which interested him, and which he determined to discover, if only for his personal satisfaction, and to justify himself. There was the truth about the attack on Defoe, also – surely he wanted to find the attacker?

He was not so sure.

He felt, as he looked across the room at Bright, that his

chief interest had died with the capture of Iris Brent. Instinctively he knew that attitude would not be long-lived, but it did not encourage him to enjoy the next few minutes.

Then Bright's attitude intrigued him.

Not until the policeman had said that there was nothing more the Toff could do had he brought out his trump card. Clearly he wanted to take the Toff off his guard; Bright probably felt that handling the Toff was not the difficult task which Scotland Yard – and the Press – so often inferred.

Rollison stirred himself.

"Congratulations," he said mildly. "I suppose I mustn't ask where you found her?"

"Near Staines," said Bright promptly. "She's on her way here now, and I'd like you to identify her."

"You did suggest that there was nothing more I could do, so I could be awkward and obstinate," said Rollison. "But at the moment I won't. How long do you think she will be?"

"I expect her by twelve o'clock."

"It's now 11.30 – I'll be here at noon sharp. Are you having an identification parade?"

"I don't think it will be necessary," said Bright complacently. "There's no charge preferred against her yet." He pushed his chair back, and went as far as to offer cigarettes. "After this, I hope I won't have to worry you, Mr. Rollison. I'm sure you're feeling the need for a rest. The blow on the head, Dr. Whittaker tells me, might have unfortunate consequences." He smiled widely, and the Toff would gladly have kicked him, although he admitted that Bright deserved his triumph.

Guildford High Street was busy. Rollison had some coffee, pondered yet more about the case and then, from a telephone-kiosk, called the *Daily Echo*. That national daily had on its staff a youthful and eager reporter, Lett by name, who would gladly co-operate with the Toff. Lett, moreover, was in the office, a rare thing for the morning.

"Rollison?" he said, and then with emphasis: "Oh, Rollison! Yes, I'm free for the day – nothing very special has come in. What are you after now?"

"You've heard about the Defoe business?"

"That breach case?" Lett sounded rather disappointed. "Yes, I have. I'm not covering it – one of our men is on the way there now."

"The angle! want covered is the girl's employer," said Rollison. "It's very hush-hush, isn't it? Arnold Crossfield – or didn't you know?"

Lett paused for a moment.

"There's nothing particularly hush-hush about it. We're making a habit of not mentioning names unless there's a direct bearing on the case. Crossfield – did you say you want his angle followed? What *is* his angle?"

"That's what I want to know."

"Look here, Rollison, are you putting something across me? There's nothing to indicate that Crossfield's concerned in this at all. Or is there?"

Rollison chuckled.

"That's exactly my own frame of mind – find what you can, will you? I hope to be in London this afternoon, or at the latest tomorrow morning."

He rang off, and then walked back to the police station. He had driven in alone, and his Frazer Nash was parked outside the station yard. As he arrived, another car drew up, and from it stepped two plain-clothes men and a girl. He did not feel any interest in the girl until she had been taken inside. Then he frowned, and quickened his step.

Bright kept him waiting for five minutes, and then, when he was ushered into the office, the girl was sitting there. She was poised, and defiant – but she did not look afraid.

She returned Rollison's even gaze steadily.

Bright said:

"Now, Mr. Rollison. Miss Brent has made a statement which confirms yours, and she has been able to account for her movements yesterday lunch-time – until six o'clock, in fact." Bright was almost urbane. "She quite understands the difficulty we have to face, and is willingly co-operating."

"Oh," said Rollison. And hastily. "Good."

"Moreover, she can give us some information about what happened yesterday," said Bright. "She was taken away in a car by the men who attacked you, and spent the night in a house in Staines. She was able to escape, and she reported immediately to the nearest policeman. Her description of the man who showed a firearm might help you to remember what happened more clearly. Would you mind repeating what you told me, Miss Brent?"

The girl said slowly, and in a tense voice:

"It was a very pale-faced man, rather under medium height. He had a scar on his upper lip – on the right side. He was going grey, although his hair was dark where it retained its colour. He had on a dark-grey suit."

She spoke as if repeating a lesson carefully rehearsed, and Rollison sat against the arm of the one easy chair in the office; she had preferred to take a stiff-backed chair.

"I don't know that it refreshes my memory much," he said. "The man was pale-faced, yes, I didn't notice the scar –" He paused, and then took out his cigarette-case. "But, as I've said, I'm very hazy about it."

"He certainly hit you hard," said the girl.

"And I shall remember it if and when I see him again," smiled Rollison. He proffered cigarettes, and she took one. Her nails were brightly polished, and coloured pink. She was wearing the dress he had seen on the previous evening; there was no doubt about that.

She let smoke curl from her nostrils.

"I'm awfully sorry to have been the cause of any trouble for you," she said. "And it was good of you to offer to help me if you could."

"Did I do that?" asked Rollison, and he smiled again.

"Your memory must have been deranged more than we thought," said Bright sarcastically, and he pushed his chair back. Rollison shrugged, bowed to the girl, nodded to Bright, whose return nod was an obvious dismissal, and went down for his car. He took it as far as the High Street, and then telephoned the Hall. After a short delay he was speaking to Jolly.

"Come here in a hurry," said Rollison. "The turning off the High Street near the police station. Is that clear?"

"I'll start at once, sir."

Jolly wasted no time in asking questions, but closed down. Rollison watched the police headquarters, and waited for some twenty-five minutes. The girl did not come from the police station, but Jolly arrived, driving a car borrowed fom Mary Crossfield.

"I hope I am in good time, sir." He spoke as the Toff stepped to him, and before he had put on the hand-brake.

"So do I," said Rollison. "Jolly, what we thought was complicated was simple. Perfectly simple, compared with what we've got now. A girl calling herself Iris Brent is at the police station, and she's got Bright eating out of her hand. She is likely to come out at any time. Follow her. On your life, don't lose her – I must find where she goes."

"Very good, sir. Did you say 'calling herself' Miss Brent?"

"I did," said Rollison slowly. "If she is Iris Brent, the girl I saw last night wasn't. This one smokes as if she's a twenty-a-day smoker. Miss Brent – my Miss Brent – didn't

70

enjoy a cigarette, and certainly isn't a habitual smoker. This girl's hands are square; my Miss Brent's were very long and narrow. This girl's hair was permed recently; my Miss Brent's wasn't, or I'm badly mistaken."

Jolly said, "Are they otherwise alike, sir?"

"Yes and no. No one who knew them well would possibly confuse them. We've got to find the other girl, Jolly, and we've got to find her quickly."

"I'll do everything I can, sir."

Jolly left the car where he had parked it and walked towards the police station. Rollison went then to the hospital, to be told that Mr. Defoe was comfortable but was not allowed to receive visitors; that was on the instructions of the police.

"Supposing I was a relative?" said Rollison.

"You would have to get police permission to see him, sir."

Rollison accepted that verdict, and then drove back to the Hall, his mind seething with the new development. It set the wheel moving almost too quickly for comfort, and too often he forgot his side and his bandaged head. Before he could do much he had to have more information about the real Iris Brent – he had also to decide which of them was the genuine Iris. An impersonation on the part of the girl whom the police were questioning would surely be the most brazen act imaginable. The risks involved would be considerable. The likeness was there, but certainly not so clear as to fool anyone who knew her reasonably well.

Had 'his' girl lied?

That seemed the obvious supposition; she could have done so and he had no way of checking, at the time, whether she told the truth or not. He had assumed that it was the truth when he had found her waiting for him. But there were other things to confuse him – her description of the gunman

71

for one. The gunman had been pale-faced, but there the accuracy of her word-picture had finished. He had been black-haired, without a streak of grey; he had been tall; there had been no scar on his upper lip.

"And so she lied," he told himself when he pulled up outside the Hall. "Bright's so damned pleased at putting one over on me that he's swallowed her whole. I hope to heaven *she's* all right," he added to himself, and he was thinking of the girl to whom he had talked after finding Defoe. "And how am I going to get a word with the victim? I –"

The front door was opened by a footman, and as he went through he heard a voice which he did not recognize. It was a man's, rather deep, and certainly authoritative. And the matter of what he was saying gave a clue to his identity.

"I have to say again, William, that your interest in your own business is so trifling that it makes me seriously perturbed about your future. You are hardly the arbiter of what metings are necessary and what are not."

Bill Crossfield's voice held a stubborn note.

"I saw no reason for going to London yesterday, and I don't see one now. There was none of this nonsense when my father was alive."

"Bill, please –" A woman's voice, Lady Crossfield's, faded away. Arnold Crossfield, plainly identified by the younger Crossfield's manner, spoke more sharply.

"Your father assumed that you would grow out of the habit of wasting time and money. You show no sign of doing either. Your behaviour in every way is unsatisfactory – you appear to consider a trifling game more important than an organization built laboriously over many years. You must alter – and you *will* alter."

The footman had disappeared. The voices were coming from the drawing-room. Rollison heard a faint sound near

72

the stairs, and saw Mary looking towards him, obviously concerned.

Bill's voice was thick with anger.

"Oh, I will, will I? I'd like to know who gave you the right to order me here, order me there! My God, I'm sick to death of it, I won't stand for it! Shut up!" he shouted, and that suggested that Arnold had tried to speak. "I've listened to you a damned sight too much, it's time you did some listening. You'll threaten to cut my allowance out altogether – all right, it's *my* money, you can't stop me taking it in a year's time. And I'll sell every tuppenny-ha'penny share I've got in the lousy business – it makes me sick! Money, money, money, that's all you think of. Have you ever taken a few hours off for relaxation? No, you're too mean, you'd be afraid to lose a penny. Before I'd grow into a money-worshipping megalomaniac I'd kill myself! I'm finished with Crossfield & Company. I'd rather be an office-boy in another firm than a guinea-pig director in my own. And I'm not joking. Get out of my way."

A heavy footstep followed, and then Mary came hurrying down the stairs.

"Rolly, don't let him go. Don't let him –"

The drawing-room door opened. Bill Crossfield came out like a bull at a gate. Rollison doubted whether he saw the others in the hall. He was white, except for a spot of red burning on either cheek, and his eyes were glittering. He went towards the front door, fumbling twice before he opened it, and hurried down the steps. He went at the same pace along the drive, his hair blowing in a slight wind; and then he fell over.

Just like that: he fell, with no apparent cause. Nor did he get up, although once or twice he tried to move.

From the far end of the drive, from a car out of sight, there came the hum of an engine.

CHAPTER TEN

Into Action

THE Toff went into action.

He turned towards the door, speaking as he went, heedless of the fact that the sudden movement was painful.

"Get him into the house, and send for Whittaker."

He did not wait to make sure that the girl had heard him, but raced down the steps and to his own car, still outside. He had turned it towards the drive when he had parked it thinking he would soon be leaving for London. He vaulted over the back of it, slid into the driving-seat and was on the move before Mary had reached the foot of the steps.

He glanced at Bill Crossfield as he passed the youngster.

Bill's eyes were opened; in them was an expression akin to surprise. On his trouser-leg there was a dark patch, and on the back of one hand a patch of red. He shouted something which Rollison did not hear.

The engine of the other car was drowned by the Frazer Nash, but Rollison saw it through the trees: it turned right, towards Guildford. He had gained twenty yards by the time he reached the end of the drive.

In another five minutes, on the clear road, he saw the first car. It was a Mini-Cooper and was travelling at a good speed. But the Frazer Nash, opened full out, swiftly reduced the distance.

There were two people in the Mini – the driver and a passenger. The Toff saw the passenger turn, and caught a glimpse of something glinting in the sun. A split-second afterwards a sharp crack echoed near him, and he saw a small hole drilled in the windscreen a foot or more from his head. He leaned forward a little, to make himself a less-conspicuous target, but no other bullets touched the larger car.

Fifty yards were between them.

Forty – thirty – twenty.

Neither the man at the wheel nor the passenger looked towards him then. They had used what ammunition they had, or they would have continued shooting. He wondered what gun they had used, for there had been no sound of a shot when Bill had fallen.

A sharp bend in the road hid them from sight for a moment. He took the bend widely, guessing that they would try to force him into the hedge, but he did not guess as well as he might. They had braked abruptly, and the Mini was slithering across the road. One man was already jumping from it; a second was standing up, behind the wheel. The Toff put on the brakes slowly, and he felt the tyres gripping, the second man jumped from the smaller car.

That was out of control.

It was travelling at no more than five miles an hour, and it crashed nose first against the hedge. Then it lurched backwards, so that for a moment it looked as if there was no way in which the Toff could avoid it. He slid the nose of the Frazer Nash towards the opposite bank, where the two men were running. He thought, even in that moment, that one was the little shrivelled man he had seen on the previous evening.

He passed the Mini safely.

It had turned on its side, and was a danger to any traffic coming along the road, but he did not think of casual motorists just then. He pulled in close to the bank, and climbed up it; the Frazer Nash being an open car, that was easy. It was not hard going, and when he reached the top of the bank he saw that his quarry were keeping together.

One *was* the shrivelled man.

It was one of those moments when Rollison would have given a lot to have a gun in his pocket, but he had gone to the Hall unarmed, expecting nothing but a quiet week-end. He went forward without hesitating, making quicker progress than the others. He was contemplating the chances of putting them out if he did get at close quarters, when one of them fell, stumbling over a tree-root.

His companion made a greater effort and, on an easier patch of ground, increased the distance between them. The fallen quarry was the little man, who grabbed a piece of a broken bough and pushed it forward to try to trip the Toff. Rollison jumped over it, but the jump made him unsteady, and the pain that went through his side when he landed was not pleasant. He grunted. The man ahead was near a low hedge, and he leapt over it and then began to run over a field on the far side.

Rollison turned.

The little man was scrambling to his feet, and there was a blaze of anger in his small brown eyes. He had clung to the tree-branch, and he used it as a weapon. Rollison side-stepped a sweeping blow. He did not feel like giving quarter, and his first punch rattled the shrivelled one's teeth. The second, to the stomach, brought him forward with a chin presented so that a miss was impossible.

Rollison clipped him, hard.

The man's teeth snapped together; he sagged, and then fell backwards, with his eyes closed and his mouth wide open. He was not prepossessing at the best of times, and he was positively ugly then. Rollison knew that he would be out for five minutes or more, and so, breathing heavily, hurried to the hedge.

The field on the other side was a small one; the man who had escaped was out of sight, and to follow him would be a waste of time. Slowly Rollison returned to his victim, seeing no sign of consciousness. He rested for some minutes, breathing heavily, and then ran through the other's pockets. He transferred a wallet and some grimy papers to his own, and eyed a long piece of string with satisfaction.

He had decided what to do the moment he had realized that only one man would come his way. He was heedless of the discomfort that the exertions had given him and, going down on one knee, he made a sound job of binding the little man's wrists. Then with the man's own dirty handkerchief he bound his ankles, and with a clean one gagged him.

The shrivelled man's eyes flickered.

Rollison lifted him, grunting with the effort, and carried him farther into the wooded patch. Bramble and hawthorn grew in abundance, but what he was looking for was a dip in the ground, and some loose fern or long grass. He found a patch of fern at last, and rolled his victim into it. By then the other was wriggling convulsively.

Rollison saw that nothing of the man himself showed at a distance of ten yards. He stripped a piece of bark from a small oak tree growing near by, and then he walked slowly back to the bank which he had climbed.

A car-engine sounded not far away, the first that he had heard since the start of the chase. It was coming from the Hall, and he was not surprised to see a car turn out of the drive; there were three men in it, all servants. The driver slowed down when he caught sight of Rollison, who called:

"They got away, across the fields. Is there any chance of catching them?"

"Not much," said a burly man, with obvious disappointment. "Are you all right, sir?"

"I'll do." Rollison went down the bank cautiously, and drew level with them. "Look after that Mini, will you? What's been happening in the Hall?"

77

"I don't rightly know, sir," said the burly speaker. "Miss Mary told us to follow you, and so we did."

"It's bad luck they didn't stick to the road," said Rollison. "I'll 'phone the police from the house," he added, and climbed into the Frazer Nash.

Within ten minutes he had telephoned the police, leaving a message, since Bright was not there. Then, for the first time, he was able to assess the situation at the Hall. That was simple, for Mary and her mother were with Bill, who had been taken at once to his own room on a stretcher, Rollison was told by a maid. Dr. Whittaker was on the way, and Mr. Arnold Crossfield was in the drawing-room.

Rollison went in.

His curiosity about Crossfield, already considerable, was the greater now. The man's reaction to what had happened would surely be interesting.

He was standing by open french windows, looking out, a tall man, broad across the shoulders, stooping a little. He was dressed in a black coat and striped morning trousers. When he turned, Rollison's impression of breadth increased; Arnold Crossfield had the ponderous build of a man run to seed. His face was florid, his features heavy, his hair thick and wiry. His eyebrows, untrimmed, gave him a fierce appearance. His lips, fleshy and not well-shaped, parted when he saw the Toff, who caught the reflection of the sun on the diamond ring which Crossfield used to fasten his cravat.

Heavy-lidded grey eyes regarded Rollison.

"And who are you?" The voice was more controlled than when he had talked to Bill Crossfield; its harshness was not so noticeable. As he spoke he put his hands behind his back, clasping them there, in the manner of a man used to making speeches and automatically falling into a platform or board-room manner.

Rollison said evenly.

"My name is Rollison."

"Presumably you are another of the witless and feckless young men who find that the ever-present hospitality of Crossfield Hall is an attraction too great to be resisted," Crossfield suggested sarcastically.

Rollison raised his eyebrows.

"Obviously Bill was right," he said. "I thought he was a little unjust, but getting along with you obviously wouldn't be easy." He slid his cigarette-case from his pocket, and offered it. Crossfield ignored it. Rollison lit a cigarette, while the old man rasped:

"Has my nephew had the impertinence to discuss me with you and his clap-trap friends?"

"I don't like your manner," said Rollison evenly. "But I can asure you – no. Yet even he couldn't help giving the impression that you made life unnecessarily difficult for him."

"Your impertinence is typical of his."

"You haven't really got to know me yet," said Rollison, keeping his temper with an effort. "Did you know that your nephew had been shot?"

"That has no bearing –"

"That should have considerable bearing on any issue concerning him," Rollison said coldly. "Your self-interest appears to have no decent limit. You *did* infer that you liked blunt speaking, didn't you?" He moved across the room, and Crossfield snapped:

"What are you doing?"

"I'm about to telephone the police."

"Will that be necessary?"

"It's usual in cases of attempted murder," said Rollison, and he saw Crossfield start.

"Are you in your right mind?"

"May I ask the same question?" asked Rollison, lifting

79

the receiver. "Guildford police station, please ... is Inspector Bright there yet? ... All right, thank you. Tell him the matter at the Hall is urgent ... Yes, urgent ... I don't know yet whether it is connected with the Defoe case."

He was watching Crossfield as he spoke, and he saw the man start again. He replaced the receiver, and sat on the table holding the telephone which he had used solely to mention 'Defoe' indirectly. He surveyed the older man in silent until Crossfield demanded:

"What right have you to behave as if you owned this house?"

"A rudimentary sense of public duty and social decency," said Rollison. "You should try to get acquainted with them both, they have their uses. And now don't you think this slanging match has gone far enough?"

"Young man," said Arnold Crossfield, and to do him justice he had recovered his equanimity very well, "this 'slanging match', as you like to call it, is an intolerable piece of impertinence on your part. Kindly leave this house immediately."

Rollison said:

"Is that a considered request?"

"It is an order."

"I may be wrong," said Rollison slowly, "and I may be right. On the whole, I think the latter wins. On the question of whether you're making a mistake or not, I mean. I think you are, only time will tell. I am very interested in the attempted murders of (a) Patrick Defoe, and (b) William Crossfield. There is a connection between them, and I propose to find what it is."

He walked towards the door as he spoke, and then turned the handle. He heard Crossfield's heavy breathing, but he was half-way into the hall when Crossfield spoke.

"Just a moment."

Rollison turned.

"You gave me an 'order' just now, didn't you?"

"I think that can be postponed," said Crossfield evenly. "I\would like to talk to you, Mr. – er – what did you say your name was?"

"Rollison."

"Mr. Rollison. You obviously suffer from delusions – you are the young man whose memory has been affected by a blow over the head, aren't you? There can be no connection between my nephew and the man Defoe, of course – no connection at all."

Although he spoke with authority and assurance, there was a tension about his manner which Rollison saw clearly – and which, in fact, he had deliberately tried to create. Rollison hesitated, then walked steadily into the passage, closing the door behind him.

As he entered the hall, he pulled up sharply, for a girl was coming in by the front door – the girl he classified as the second Iris Brent.

CHAPTER ELEVEN

Which is Which?

SHE came in briskly, and in a faintly nasal voice said:

"Tell Mr. Crossfield I'm here, please."

It was the first time that Rollison had heard her speak naturally; at the police station she had been considering both her words and the way she uttered them. Now she smiled at Rollison, with a touch almost of insolence in her expression.

From her "tell Mr. Crossfield I'm here, please", and the maid's immediate acceptance of it, Rollison knew she was no stranger to the Hall. As he approached her he remembered that when she had arrived at the Guildford police station he had not given her a second thought until after she had disappeared from his sight. He had only seen her back, and nothing about it had reminded him of the girl he had first known as Iris Brent.

Nor was there anything about this girl's figure to remind him of the other girl.

There was no difference which could be easily defined. They were about the same height and figure, but their carriage, their way of bearing themselves, was entirely different. Instinctively he had thought of the original Iris as "county". The same thought did not strike him as he eyed the woman in the hall.

"I didn't expect to see you here," she said.

There could have been a double meaning in that, although Rollison wondered if he were taking an inference which was not there. It was possible to infer from her words that she had expected Crossfield would soon get rid of him. On the other hand, it may have been a casual remark, made for something to say.

"Didn't you?" He spoke lightly. "You nearly weren't surprised, since I'm on my way out."

The drawing-room door opened, revealing Crossfield. Rollison had an idea that the man had stayed by the door, listening; at least there was no sound from it when it opened, although he had heard a handle turn when the maid had come away after giving her message.

"Good morning, Miss Brent." Crossfield had complete control of himself. "Go to my library, will you, and I will come up in a few minutes. Mr. Rollison, may I have a word with you?"

Rollison had left the man solely to test the depth of his wish to talk. Unless it were deep, he would allow Rollison to go to the devil, for certainly he had been treated in a cavalier fashion unlikely to please him. After Rollison's deliberate exit from the drawing-room, nine men in ten would have avoided a talk. Crossfield was eager for one; and that must mean he was particularly anxious to make sure that the impression of a connection between the attack on Defoe and that on Bill was not spread about.

Rollison stepped back to the drawing-room. Iris Brent went upstairs, taking her gloves off as she walked. Crossfield stood aside for Rollison to pass, and when they were in the room he smiled. It was an attractive smile, robbing the man of the fierceness which his appearance first suggested. Moreover, he had firm white teeth – natural, Rollison judged.

"Now, Mr. Rollison, let us understand each other. I can quite realize that as a friend of my nephew you were quick to defend him. If your manner was abrupt, I will overlook it – my own, perhaps, was not beyond reproach."

"No offence taken or intended," murmured Rollison.

"Excellent – and please smoke, if you wish. No thanks, I neither smoke nor drink alcohol." He waited for Rollison to light a cigarette. "Your idea that my nephew's accident and Defoe's injury had any association is quite out of question, as I said before. May I ask whether you had any reason for connecting them?"

Rollison said: " 'Accident' hardly covers either mishap, do you think? They were deliberate attacks, and when two crimes of violence take place in the same vicinity within so short a space of time, the probability of a connection is quite strong."

"Is that the limit of your reasoning?"

"Is there a limit to reasoning?"

"Don't let us continue at cross-purposes," said Crossfield, testily. "Had you any particular cause for suggesting that

83

the two – er – incidents might not be entirely separate?"

Rollison leaned against the arm of the chair and made a great show of sharing a confidence.

"I don't really see why I should pass this on to you, Mr. Crossfield, but seeing that your nephew is involved, it might perhaps be wise." He spoke formally, almost stiltedly, to match the older man, and also to emphasize his seriousness. "At least one peculiar factor emerged. Yesterday, after I was driven back from Defoe's cottage by Dr. Whittaker, a Mini-Cooper car followed me. I noticed the number – EX21. The car in which Bill's assailants made off had the same number."

Crossfield's brows contracted; his shaggy eyebrows tangled together.

"Did they, indeed! Then I can quite see your point of view, Mr. Rollison, but I do hope that you will jump to no conclusions. I believe" – he smiled again, in the manner of a man of position deliberately and consciously coming down to the level of a subordinate who should be humoured – "that you have some kind of a hobby – I might almost say reputation."

Rollison smiled. "My reputation seems to have gone well ahead of me, but I wouldn't call it a hobby."

"No?" Crossfield remained polite.

"No," repeated the Toff. "I take it very seriously indeed, Mr. Crossfield. I am one of the few people who has been left more money than is needed. You might say that your nephew and I have something in common! At all events, crime fascinated me, and I studied it, not always from a distance. One might say it is my only profession – a study of crime, and the ways of combating it. Defoe's wound was curious in many respects. Other features in the case were intriguing and the latest development makes me very curious indeed."

84

Crossfield positively purred.

"It is refreshing to know that you have so high a motive, Mr. Rollison – if only we could reduce crime to an absolute minimum, how much happier this world would be! But in the present instance, don't you think that you are, perhaps, interesting yourself in a matter which might best be left alone?"

"I haven't thought so yet," said Rollison.

"I wish you would consider that point of view," said Crossfield. "So many distressing things might be avoided – my secretary's unfortunate part in Defoe's life, for instance, has already received publicity enough."

Rollison said slowly:

"I can't stop the publicity. The Press will be after this in full cry."

"Of course. But they can be handled with discretion. I am thinking of your interest more than that of newspapers."

"I wonder why."

The shaggy brows drew together again.

"The matter surely affects me? The stubborn attitude of my nephew is disturbing enough, and this peculiar attack on him will not make my position easier."

Rollison smiled. "No. Unfortunately I'm as obstinate as Bill."

Crossfield said sharply:

"I hope you are not."

"I always have been," said Rollison. "My curiosity positively gets out of hand. Now I'm wondering why you want to get rid of me and to arrange for me to take no further interest. Had you asked whether I could help you to discover the motive of the attack it would have been more understandable, don't you think?"

Crossfield bunched his hands together, but kept his temper.

"I can see that we are not going to reach an agreement, Mr. Rollison."

"Well, at least we're agreed in that," smiled the Toff. "My angle is your nephew's, of course."

Crossfield shrugged.

"It is a pity, but" – he stepped towards the door. – "I can see no object in pursuing the subject further. Good day, Mr. Rollison. Oh –" he went on again as they stepped into the hall: "If you find it more convenient to go in the morning, please stay overnight."

"Thank you," said Rollison. "You're very kind."

He intended to move from Crossfield Hall before the day was out, but he did not reject the amended "order" out of hand. It might prove useful to spend another night at the Hall, although he doubted whether Crossfield would make it easy for him to do more than use his room and the living rooms. Crossfield's antagonism was a thing which was quite beyond doubt, but that was not the only intriguing factor.

He was no fool; but he had advanced foolish reasons for wanting Rollison to take no further interest. He had been very anxious indeed to learn why Rollison associated the two crimes. Doubtless he thought he knew the reason; Rollison wondered what he would have thought had he known of the shrivelled little man bundled up and hidden in the fern and gorse not half a mile away.

"If he isn't Suspect Number One, he's precious near it," Rollison mused aloud, and then he smiled. "Suspected of what? What *is* behind it?"

He was not likely to find, at that moment, any satisfactory answer, and in any case, there were many things to be done. He wanted a word with Jolly, who had doubtless followed Iris Brent at a safe distance. He went to his room, and found his man waiting by the window, looking over the parkland of the Hall.

"Hallo," said Rollison amiably. "Enjoying the view?"

"It is a delightful one, sir, but I have more pressing things on my mind. I wish to report that I followed Miss Brent to this residence. I have made enquiries below – apparently she is here whenever Mr. Arnold Crossfield is. Three servants saw her arrive, and none had any doubt at all of her identity. In fact, one of them – the housekeeper, who has a somewhat Victorian outlook – disapproves strongly of her heavy smoking. You mentioned something about that, I believe, sir."

"Ye-es," said Rollison, and slowly, "so this *is* Iris Brent."

"There can be no reasonable doubt about that, sir."

"And after one look at her, you wouldn't be surprised that she figured in a breach-of-promise case?"

"No. Nor that she could be – er – bought off, if the financial inducement were strong enough."

"Again, yes," said Rollison. He sat on the bed slowly. "There's no false romance about this Iris. The girl I saw yesterday might have been persuaded by Defoe to withdraw, but Crossfield's secretary would reckon strictly in terms of £ s. d. Jolly, Mr. Crossfield doesn't want me to be interested. You've heard of Mr. William's trouble, no doubt."

"Yes, sir. It is most bewildering."

"We're in full agreement," admitted Rollison. "Well, go into the village, and find a man named Wally Simm. I don't know which cottage he lives in, but you'll probably find him in it. Ask him to meet me on the road leading to Defoe's cottage in an hour's time. In fact, go with him."

"Very well, sir."

"And ask him also if he knows of an empty gardener's shed – anywhere, in fact, where we might keep a man for a

87

day or two without harming the man or the premises."

Jolly's eyes did not flicker.

"Very good, sir. Is there anything else?"

"Not just now," said Rollison.

He was, by then, getting worried about the girl of the cottage. That Iris Brent had lied, that she had deliberately told the police that she had been to the cottage and talked with Rollison – having, of course, heard that she was suspected of so doing – was beyond question. Whether she really believed that Rollison was deceived by her appearance was a different matter.

If she knew the other girl, and was aware of some likeness, she might think that she could get past him. Her manner at the police station had shown anxiety – as if she had been prepared for a disclaimer, and yet afraid of the need for it.

Then he grew aware of another queer thing; the photograph that Bright had shown him had surely been of the girl he had first met. He had, at all events, thought so. True, with make-up and a few touches here and there, it would have covered either girl.

"It gets more involved as time goes on," he said aloud, and then he waited for Jolly to return, and for the meeting with Wally Simm. After that meeting he hoped he would have a hiding-place for his prisoner; and he believed the man could be persuaded to talk. To find the missing girl was essential, but if the prisoner would not talk, then the real Iris Brent might be a readier subject for interrogation.

He would certainly have thought so had he known what was in the mind of Crossfield's secretary as she waited for her employer.

Crossfield entered his library – or his late brother's library – and closed the door carefully. He said at once:

"Was Rollison deceived?"

"You needn't worry about that," said Iris Brent confidently. "He couldn't have seen much of her, so she didn't have a lot of time for talking."

"That is just as well," said Crossfield, and he drew a breath of relief. "It has been a most unfortunate development, my dear. Rollison is being a nuisance."

"You can handle him," she said with assurance.

"It is to be hoped," said Arnold Crossfield. He was silent for some minutes, and then shrugged. "He is leaving tonight or tomorrow morning, and I hope that will be the last we hear of him. It will be wise, I think, to send William to a nursing-home – he isn't wanted here."

"Is he wanted at all?" inquired Iris Brent.

CHAPTER TWELVE

Little Shrivelled Man

JOLLY turned into the narrow path leading to a cottage at the east end of Fern Cross. The cottage was pleasing to the eye, with a new thatch on the roof, ramblers over the porch, a neatly kept front garden, and a vegetable patch at the back. It was detached, although it stood only a few yards from four equally well-tended cottages nearer the middle of the village.

Jolly, immaculate in black clothes, pale-faced and sombre of countenance, knocked on the front door and stood back two yards. After a pause and a bustle of footsteps, a plump, red-faced woman opened the door, looking at the caller with surprised concern.

"Well! I thought it were the baker."

"I am sorry to disappoint you, madam," said Jolly

soberly. "May I have the pleasure of a word with Mr. Simm?"

"Well, you'll have to wait," she said. "Wally never likes being disturbed at his after-dinner nap. Would you come in? – he won't be long."

"I will take full responsibility for disturbing him, madam," said Jolly grandiloquently.

"When you've been married to Wally Simm for twenty-nine years, you don't wake him after dinner!" declared Mrs. Simm roundly. "But you can wait in the parlour." She stood aside for Jolly to pass, not knowing that it was one of the rare occasions in his life when Jolly was nonplussed. He squeezed past her, and went straight along the passage, instead of to the left where she indicated an open door.

"Not that way!" called Mrs. Simm urgently.

Jolly half turned, and was then seized with a paroxysm of coughing surely enough to waken the dead. He saw Mrs. Simm begin to show alarm. He heard a chair scrape not far ahead of him. He began to apologize, but before he had gone far the kitchen door opened to emit a pleasant smell of baking cakes, and a wrathful Wally. Wally had loosened his collar and tie, his greying hair was dishevelled, and there was evidence of sleep in his eyes.

That Wally was a dictator in his own home was clear. That the countryman was also the village poacher, and spent many of his nights abroad, was not. Had Jolly been aware of that he might have considered waiting, for poachers by night need sleep by day.

"Lizzie!" roared Wally Simm. "Lizzie, where are ye – oh, there you be, hidin' behind the door – didn't I tell you I wasn't to be woke up? Do I have to tell 'ee that *every* afternoon I has a nap?"

Jolly squeezed in two words.

"The fault –"

"Ne'er mind whose fault it were. Lizzie knows I don't be woke when I'm havin' me after-dinner sleep!" roared Wally. "If it ain't to help her wi' the mangle it's to get coal in, bother the woman." He was cooling down, but he regarded Jolly with a somewhat fiery interest.

"The fault was *entirely* mine," said Jolly. "Mrs. Simm impressed on me most emphatically the need for allowing you to rest, but an unfortunate –"

"Who are you?" demanded Wally.

"My name is Jolly. I have come –"

"I'm not int'rested in *anything*," declared Wally with aggressive certainty. "In *anything*, you understand. Lizzie, I'm goin' to have a nap, and you'll know all about it if I'm woke again." He turned back to the kitchen, with Jolly positively out of countenance.

"But – er – but, Mr. Simm, Mr. Rollison –"

Wally turned sharply.

"Who?"

"Mr. Rollison asked me to call on you."

"How long have you been waitin'?" demanded Wally, aggressiveness quite gone. "Come in, now, come in. Lizzie, why wasn't I told the minnit the gentleman come?" He ushered Jolly into the kitchen, a tiny place where a fire was burning despite the warmth of the June day. The smell of cooking came from an old coal-fired oven. The kitchen was as clean as a proverbial new pin, the walls covered with pictures, bric-à-brac and photographs. The latticed windows were highly polished and chintz curtains hung on either side of them.

Two old saddle-back chairs were by the fire.

"Sit ye down," said Wally Simm, "and tell me all about un."

Lizzie Simm bustled through the kitchen to the scullery, and Wally stretched out a hand to give her bottom a gentle pat, winking as he did so. She tossed her head, but was smiling broadly when she shut the two men in together. Jolly drew a deep breath, and gave his message.

"We'm best be goin'," said Wally, after two or three minutes. "Wait while I put on me tie." He did so, in front of a small mirror on the low mantelshelf, and outside hesitated when he saw the car, which Jolly had parked a little farther up the road.

"Another o' *them* things," he said disparagingly. "It aren't far to walk."

Jolly positively perspired in anticipation.

"Mr. Rollison was in a *great* hurry."

"Ar. Hurry, hurry, that's all you'm folk think about," declared Wally, but he climbed into the Frazer Nash, which Jolly had taken for the journey, and was driven at speed to the Hall. Wally clung on to his side tightly and tensely, and Jolly, after five minutes, felt that he had not only taken his revenge, but had recovered his poise, which had not been so shaken for a long time.

Jolly took the poacher to the belt of trees near Defoe's cottage. A policeman was on duty there, but although he must have heard the car he could not see it. Also at speed, Jolly returned to the Hall, and collected Rollison, who had lunched with Mary and learned from her that she disliked Iris Brent as cordially as she did her uncle.

No mention had been made of Defoe.

In something under fifteen minutes from the time of leaving the table, Rollison stepped out of the car and met Simm again. The poacher looked up at him with a crooked grin.

"Here I am, sir."

"And in good time," said Rollison. "Jolly's told you what I want?"

"I know just the place, sir – just the very place. A little

gamekeeper's hut, it be, hidden in a copse, no one'll be there this side've July, seein' they're not using the copse this season comin'. I knows it well," added Wally.

"Good man. And you realize what you're doing?"

"Aye Don't worry about *me*, sir."

As he drove back with the two men Rollison wondered what there was in Defoe to inspire liking in Mary Crossfield and her brother, and such loyalty in Wally Simm.

Wally's help was invaluable from the time they neared the drive. He knew of a cart-track which would take them into the wooded patch where the prisoner was waiting, so that the car could get close, and yet not be seen from the main road. He showed no surprise at all when the little shrivelled man was located, and Jolly carried him to the car. Once or twice he chuckled; it was as if this was an adventure after Wally's own heart.

In an hour they were in the gamekeeper's hut.

It was well-kept, and freshly creosoted; nothing on the Crossfield estate was allowed to be dilapidated, as Rollison could see. The prisoner was conscious, sullen, obviously more than a little scared.

Rollison asked:

"How far from here could a shout be heard, Wally?"

"There aren't much chance o' *that*," said Wally, and he leered at the prisoner. "Depends on the shout, mind you."

"Ye-es," said Rollison. "I shouldn't think he has a loud voice, would you?" He bent down and unfastened the handkerchief which had served so well as a gag. There was a red mark on either side of the shrivelled man's mouth.

"Shrivelled" was precisely the word.

He was small, and his face was pale with the pallor of any town-dweller, not the pastiness of the man he had been with on the previous day. His little eyes, too close-set, were shifty. His clothes were too big for him, as if they had been made for a much bigger man, or he had shrunk within them. But his face was the noticeable thing – an ugly, small and wizened countenance, with the skin set in a myriad wrinkles.

He licked dry lips, and:

"You – you'll be sorry for this!"

"That shows spirit," admitted the Toff, "but I don't think you'll feel spirited for very long. You and your precious friends took a girl somewhere yesterday; and today you shot Bill Crossfield."

"What!" This from Wally, who stepped forward with his eyes positively blazing. "Shot Master Bill! Why, you –"

Rollison restrained him.

"Later, Wally, if he doesn't talk." He addressed himself to the little man. "What's your name?"

"I – I ain't talkin'."

Rollison remembered the papers he had already from the other's pocket – papers which he had not yet examined. Things had happened too quickly, and no sooner had one job cropped up for attention than another pushed it aside. He glanced through them casually. There was nothing of importance, but there were two soiled and grubby letters, both addressed in hardly decipherable writing to: *"Mr. L. Parker, 21 Gay Street, Mile End, E."*

"Up to a point, this talks for you," said Rollison. "Well, Mr. Parker, I want two things. The address where you took the girl, and the reason you shot Crossfield."

Parker set his lips tightly; there was real courage in him, after all.

"Just let me have *five* minutes with un," pleaded Wally.

"Very soon, if we go on like this," said Rollison. "Well, Parker? Are you going to talk before or after you get hurt?"

Silence followed again, broken by Wally's:

"All right, *three* minutes."

94

Rollison did not think there was much doubt that violence, even in a mild degree would loosen the man's tongue. Nor had he any particular objection to using violence in the circumstances, for the means would certainly justify the end. But he preferred to use persuasion, and he snapped:

"All right, Parker. Why knife Defoe?"

That worked: the man tried to sit up.

"I never: we found him that way!"

"All right, so you found him that way," said Rollison. "Why take the girl?"

"I – I only obey orders."

"Whose orders?"

Again there was silence, and Rollison stood aside, motioning to Wally. Wally went forward, his fists doubled. He had to bend low to get near the prisoner, whose hands and feet were still bound, and who could do nothing but strain away. There was ferocity in Wally's eyes, and a clear intention to hit and to hurt.

Then to Rollison's surprise, and the obvious fear of the prisoner, Wally stopped, unclenched one hand, and drew a clasp-knife from his pocket. He cut the string at the man's wrists, and untied the handkerchief at his ankles.

"Come on, get *up*," he snapped. "Get *up*, an' I'll put you down again. Get – up!" He shot out a hand and yanked Parker to his feet. He pushed him rather than hit him, and Parker thudded against the wooden wall of the shed, then slithered down. Wally turned his face, until then set ferociously, towards the Toff. He winked broadly. Rollison smothered a laugh, and Jolly passed a hand across his forehead; with Wally Simm he was quite out of his depth.

Wally smacked Parker's face sharply:

"You were told to *talk*, weren't you? Well, if you don't *I* know a way of makin' you, see? Now get up."

"I – I only takes orders," gasped the man named Parker.

"Lossen took the dame to a house in Staines. I'll give you the address, but take this devil orf me, mister, take 'im orf!"

CHAPTER THIRTEEN

Acknowledgements to Wally

ONCE started, Parker talked quickly.

Rollison looked at Jolly, knowing that his man was marvelling, as he was himself, at the effectiveness of Wally's methods. They were methods which the Toff had often used himself, and had called by the grandiose name of psychological terrorism; true, he had not invented the expression, but it had always pleased him.

First frighten your man –then get what you want from him.

He had applied the method a hundred times, but never more effectively than Wally Simm, who was standing against the wall of the shed and looking down with robust satisfaction.

Parker's voice was tinged with fear.

"Lossen's my boss, 'e sent me, guv'nor. He sent me an' Lew to put young Crossfield out, I never knew why. That's Gawd's truth!" He was sweating at the forehead and the back of his neck, and his eyes were staring. "We was to watch the 'all an' give Crossfield 'is."

The satisfaction went from Wally's face and Rollison looked bleak.

"So you take murder as lightly as that, do you?"

"Murder? Gawd, no!" Parker almost screeched. "Put 'im out of the way fer a bit, that's all, strike me, I never meant to kill 'im! Lossen said put 'im out ..." Parker drew

96

a deep, slobbering breath. "He's not dead, mister, he's not dead! That little pellet-shooter wouldn't kill no one!"

Rollison said:

"It would kill all right, and you know it. What was it – an air-pistol?"

"Y-yes, I never –" Parker broke off, obviously telling only part of the truth, although Rollison suspected it was true that he had not intended to kill Bill Crossfield.

"All right, forget that," said Rollison.

"Is – is he dead?"

"He's pretty near it."

"I never meant it," gasped Parker. "I never meant to croak 'im, guv'nor, Gawd, if the dicks –" Rollison had rarely seen a more objectionable show of fear. "The – the skirt you're after, guv'nor – keep the dicks away and I'll tell you where she went. Keep away!" He saw Rollison's expression, and also saw Wally step forward. He raised his voice. "I say I'll tell you! She's at 7 Ledsham Road, Staines – that's the address, you'll find her there. Lossen said she'd be all right so long as she behaved."

"Why take her at all?" demanded Rollison.

"I don't know. I only obeyed orders, I tell yer. Lossen gives the orders, 'e always 'as. 'E don't take no fer an answer. I couldn't 'elp meself, I swear it." He wiped the palm of his hand across his forehead. "Comes to me yesterd'y mornin', 'e does, me an' Lew –"

"Who is Lew?"

"Lew – Lew Garney, we string along, guv'nor, we always does. Said 'e'd got a job for us, an' brought us down 'ere. When we gets to the cottige, the fellow Defoe's got one. He'd – he'd bin patched up, so we looks arahnd –"

"What for?"

"Lossen wanted some doc – doc – *papers* or so he said."

"Did you find them?"

97

"No, I swear we never – even looked in the garden, we did – dug down where the trees was, to see if there was a box. It was Lossen's idea, Guv'nor, it's Gawd's truth, s'welp me if it wasn't. I wouldn't lie to you, I know better."

"If you lie you'll regret it," said Rollison, and he turned to Wally. He believed the story; he did not think that it was possible for Parker to show such fear as he showed then without being wholly genuine. "Is he all right here for a bit?"

"As safe as anywhere in Surrey," Wally declared. "Like I told you, sir."

"What – what're you goin' ter do?" Parker muttered.

"Leave you to brood over your sins," said Rollison. "If you've lied just once, it's the mistake of your life." He refastened the handkerchief about the man's ankles, and Jolly took a piece of cord from his pocket and rebound the wrists. Rollison put the handkerchief gag back loosely, pointing out to Wally and Jolly that if Parker shouted the police would be on the scene quickly, so that there was no need for a tight gag. Parker would not want to attract attention.

They left the shed, and Rollison told Simm that Bill Crossfield was not badly hurt. Then he added thoughtfully:

"This fellow had better have some food before night, Wally. Can you arrange that?"

"Leave un to me," said Wally. "I'll see he don't *starve*."

Rollison grinned.

"Good man! And you've been worth a dozen of Bright's coppers. I haven't seen a neater job for a long time."

Wally winked.

"Me an' the missus was readin' about you, sir – found a paper in the larder, one she covers the shelves with. Could ha' knocked me down when I see it, an' reelized who you was. What you do's all right with me, sir. But" – he grew serious, and the atmosphere changed – "do me a favour, sir – find who done that foul thing to Mr. Defoe. I don't care *what* anyone says, sir, he's a real gentleman. Always treated me that way, and say as you find, that's Wally Simm."

"All right, Wally, we'll find out what happened to Mr. Defoe, and he's all right now – the police will look after that."

Wally grimaced.

"Oh, *them*," he said. "I've read about them in the papers too."

They left him a few minutes afterwards. He preferred to walk back to the village after taking them in the Frazer Nash to a point near the road. It was not likely that they had been seen; the work being done in the coveys and copses that year was on another part of the estate, and no gamekeepers were active near the shed. Rollison did not mind the police knowing he had been to the cottage; it would, in fact, probably have puzzled them to learn that he had not gone near.

Driving back to the Hall, he said:

"We owe a lot to Simm, Jolly."

"So I perceive, sir."

"I notice a slight coolness," said Rollison.

"Mr. Simm and myself, sir, are not likely to view many things from the same perspective. However, he is a most worthy person." Jolly dismissed the countryman airily, and went on: "May I ask what you propose to do next?"

"We're going to London at once. You're stopping at Staines – I think we should borrow the car again, and drive up separately. You'll locate and watch 7 Ledsham Road, and telephone me at the flat. When you've done that I'll go to Gay Street and make some inquiries about Parker." Rollison spoke thoughtfully. "I know Gay Street well enough and 'Parker' has a familiar ring, but the little snide back there is a stranger."

"And to me, sir."

"Parker, Parker," repeated Rollison, as if to himself, and his eyes narrowed. "*Ma* Parker, Jolly. She's an old harridan living in Gay Street – she served a sentence for baby-farming before I was born; Grice was telling me about her once upon a time."

"I believe I remember you mentioning it, sir. A praiseworthy feat of memory, if I may say so."

Rollison chuckled.

"As always, you'll say what you like! Well we've learned more than I thought was likely, and we've solved the gardening puzzle. Lossen arranged to dig in easy places, assuming that doc – doc – *papers*, as Parker would say, might be hidden there. Lossen, of course, is our Pale Face, whom Crossfield's secretary picturesquely robbed of some inches in height and gave a scar to a blemishless upper lip. Where are we?"

"Approaching the Hall, sir."

"Don't be an ass. Where are we in the process of reasoning?" Rollison was, in fact, in a good temper, for he believed that he would find the girl he had first seen, and he also believed that Parker had been right when he had reported that she would not be hurt if she "behaved" herself. His good temper was kindled by relief, for if she suffered, the blame would be partly his for having failed to tell the full story to the police. Keeping facts from the police did not worry him, but he liked to be sure that no harm would fall to anyone because of it.

The day, cooler than the previous one, but fine and sunny, increased his good spirits. He had the pale-faced man's name, he had the Gay Street angle, and:

"We know that Lossen and his boy-friends didn't want

100

Defoe killed, or they would have killed him. Earlier we assumed that they hadn't knifed him, and, if Parker told the truth, they didn't. So that's where we are, Jolly – we know that someone apart from the Lossen lot knifed Defoe."

"Your young lady is a possibility, sir."

"Don't call her my young lady! And I don't want to admit at this stage that she's a possibility, Jolly. We're going to assume her innocent. So it follows that there's someone else. The second Iris could not be in love with Defoe, could she? Remember Bright said she had an alibi. Do you know, it won't surprise me if Arnold Crossfield gave her that alibi."

"It would hardly be surprising had she been working with him, sir."

"No. We'll check up as soon as we can."

They had turned into the drive, and he pulled up outside the imposing entrance to the Hall. At the back of his mind there was a growing feeling of apprehension lest some new development should prevent him from making the journey, but there was none.

At Arnold Crossfield's suggestion Bill had been sent to a nursing-home on the outskirts of Guildford. Bright had been and made inquiries. The Mini, of course, was being checked by the police. A constable – not Featherby, whom the Toff had grown to like – was on duty at the Hall.

Mary and her mother had gone out, ostensibly to do some shopping, probably to call on Bill later in the day. Rollison wished that he could see Mary for ten minutes; he was puzzled by the nursing-home development, and wondered whether there had been any particular reason for or strong objection to it. There appeared no reason why Bill, who had surely not been badly hurt, should leave the house.

Had Crossfield insisted on that?

Rollison did not see the older man, nor Iris Brent, although Jolly obtained the information that they were working in the library. Jolly had also told the Toff that Arnold Crossfield was no more popular with the servants than with the family. Moreover, what little gossip he had been able to pick up from the village suggested that Arnold received nothing like the universal respect which had been accorded his brother.

There was no difficulty in borrowing a car for Jolly, and they left the Hall ten minutes after doing so, Rollison bringing up the rear. Half-way through Fern Cross he saw a familiar car pulling into the gateway of a small Georgian house, and he recognized Whittaker. The doctor saw him, and his expression was eager as he called across the narrow High Street:

"Can you spare me a few minutes, Mr. Rollison?"

"I was going to ask you the same thing," said Rollison, and walked towards the other. "Ostensibly for you to have another look at my head, of course!"

"How is it?"

"No more than a nuisance."

"Good." They went into the house, a mellow place which reflected the character of the doctor, who led the way into a small study lined with books, most of which gave the appearance of being in frequent use. One wall was confined to medical text-books, of surprising variety. The classics and modern literature were on another. The third wall, furnished with book-shelves, contained a miscellany of crime stories, and Whittaker smiled when he saw the Toff looking at them.

"A great number of people like to be thrilled vicariously, Mr. Rollison – you're one of the few who get your thrills in fact and not fiction." The smile disappeared, and he looked a worried man. "I can't understand why Bill Crossfield has been sent to a nursing-home," he said. "He's not badly hurt.

A bullet – a slug from an air-gun, I believe – cut a tendon behind his left knee, and that crippled him. There were one or two other minor wounds, nothing at all serious. He could have been treated as well at the Hall as in a nursing-home – in fact, rather better. Yet his uncle insisted on the move."

"Crossfield was responsible, was he?" remarked Rollison. "How did the family react?"

"They didn't like it a bit. Lady Crossfield was almost in tears, but of course none of them can effectively oppose Crossfield himself. I thought you should know, Mr. Rollison."

"Thanks very much – I wanted to find out. And shall we drop the 'Mr.'?" smiled Rollison. "You've been a great help – without you and Wally I don't know where I would have been. Something of a local character, isn't he?"

"Wally Simm?" Whittaker laughed. "He's the local poacher, as you may have gathered. One of the most popular men in the village, and as straight as they're made – poaching apart, of course!" Whittaker pushed his hair back from his forehead. "Well, I've some prescriptions to make up, and some calls I mustn't leave any longer. Where are you off to?"

"To look at the London angle," said Rollison.

He shook hands and left the doctor's house, then drove fast towards London. He did not go across country towards Staines, and he did not see Jolly on the way. But he did see a small Morris which followed him from Guildford.

It had not been on the road at Fern Cross, and after it had dogged him for ten minutes he had deliberately slowed down to let it pass. The driver had not taken the opportunity, which convinced the Toff that he was being followed, and that it was not the type of job to which the man was accustomed. Had he been an expert he would have passed the Toff and allowed himself to be passed later.

103

Rollison could not see the man clearly, for the glass of the windscreen was dirty so that it was difficult to see into the interior.

When he reached London, the Morris followed him to the end of Gresham Terrace, which was near Piccadilly, and then went its own way. Rollison left the Frazer Nash outside his flat and walked to the end of the Terrace. The Morris was parked twenty yards away, and its driver was still inside.

Rollison returned to the flat; there was no purpose in taking action then. He was anxious to start the "London angle", which he felt was more important even than that of Fern Cross. He was on edge, also, to help the missing girl, and it did not seriously occur to him that he could not do so.

At five o'clock he was in his flat.

By half past five he expected word from Jolly.

By six he was growing impatient.

By seven he was worried, for it was not Jolly's habit to take a long time over a task which was, in essence, simple. But the minutes passed, and no word came.

CHAPTER FOURTEEN

Vide Press

IT was just after seven-thirty when the front door bell rang. Rollison stood up quickly from an easy chair and was prepared to greet Jolly eagerly. Instead, he saw a tall, rangy youngster, fair-haired, blue-eyed, and smiling.

"Hallo, hallo," said the newcomer, and entered without being invited. "Any news?"

Rollison covered his disappointment, seeing in Lett, the *Echo* reporter, a way out of his more urgent difficulty.

"Nothing important," he said. "Have you?"

"Yes and no." Lett helped himself to an easy chair and stretched his legs out. He had long been a frequent visitor to the flat, which was Welcome Hall to a surprising diversity of types and characters. "I've covered the Arnold Crossfield angle, as advised. It's a queer business, as you'll have guessed. Apparently Crossfield persuaded the girl to withdraw her breach case."

"Are you sure?" Rollison's voice was sharp.

"Oh, there's no doubt about it," said Lett. "I managed to get friendly with a woman in Crossfield's London office – not a big place, one used for convenience more than anything else. Anyhow, to cut a long story short, Crossfield told Iris Brent that he wasn't prepared to continue employing her if she persisted with the suit, and so it was withdrawn. I couldn't get any details, but the woman I saw heard a little of the conversation. She doesn't like Iris."

Rollison was not surprised; in fact, he had almost expected something like this. He would have been far more interested, however, but for the anxiety he felt for Jolly. He stood up and said: "Thanks, Lett. Are you busy this evening?"

The reporter grinned.

"Aren't I always out for copy?"

"I mean, can you stay here for an hour or two? I'm expecting word from Jolly, and it's late. I've a job I must do myself – nothing sensational, a mission of inquiry only. Will you stay?"

"Glad to. Conditionally, of course – that I get the first pick if and when the story breaks."

"It's yours," said Rollison. "I'll be back here within a few minutes of nine. Help yourself to anything that tempts you in the larder – you know where the beer is." He went out, leaving Lett mildly puzzled by his obvious anxiety, and drove quickly to the East End.

He was well known there.

So well known, in fact, that as the nose of the Frazer Nash reached Aldgate Pump, word began to go along Mile End Road and Commercial Road, until it spread to all corners and all places – word that the Toff was in the vicinity. Most people received the news with pleasure, for the Toff had made himself immensely popular, since he was always prepared to give the small-time crook a square deal; believing that the police did not, was the chief reason for the eagerness of the East End to bind itself together in defence of "wanted" inhabitants. The legends which existed about the Toff in that part of London were varied, but they had one thing in common.

You could trust the Toff if you played straight; and he was more dangerous than the police if you did not.

But if there were many people who liked, and respected, and admired him, there were others whose reaction was very different. At some windows as he passed men and women crouched, scowling and inwardly afraid that he had come to see them. Consciences were very uneasy when the Toff went past Aldgate Pump, and many a man scurried into hiding, believing in his heart that if the Toff really wanted to find him it would be done.

Gay Street, squalid, grey, dirty and smelly, with its great archway, part of a railway viaduct, sprawled across one end, was not empty. Blousy, big-bosomed women stood by their front doors, thin and shapeless woman talking with them. Old men and young sat on doorsteps or kitchen chairs, ostensibly sunning themselves, actually to see the Toff if he passed their way. Children up to seven played hop-scotch or kindred games on the narrow pavement, the only people genuinely to ignore him. Children of eight and over played pitch-and-toss in open defiance, a little uncertain of their wisdom and yet knowing there was nothing to fear from this legendary man.

He pulled up outside the nearest group of people.

There were five in all, and the number of the house outside which they gathered was 69, so he was well-removed from Ma Parker's.

Women smiled, men touched their caps, one enormous woman actually tucking her hair more tidily beneath a man's cloth cap, and wheezed:

"Glad to see yer, Mister Ar."

"I haven't looked you up for a long time," smiled the Toff. "How are things with you?"

"We ain't grumblin'," said the fat woman, who had to draw in a deep, asthmatic breath before each sentence, but who was an inveterate gossip. "Summer ain't so bad, Mister Ar."

The summer was the good period here; the winter the one of need and danger and difficulty. Often the Toff had helped them for the sake of helping, which was another reason why he had so many friends. He talked for a few minutes, then led the conversation to Ma Parker and her brood.

He heard two stories.

First, concerning Parker, whose Christian name was Leslie; that explained the "L. Parker" in the letters found in his pocket. Apparently Leslie Parker was the only child generally believed to have been the lawful son of Ma, born in wedlock, before her husband died and she took first to baby-farming and then to lodging-house keeping. She had had other children of her own, but few of them ever returned to Gay Street after shaking off the maternal yoke. She was a one, Ma Parker; men – you couldn't count them! She ought to have been inside a long time before she was, and then she only got one year – just like the dicks and the beaks, one year for farming kids the way she had – she should have been given a lifer.

There was only one thing about Ma Parker which really puzzled them all – that man Lossen.

Rollison let them believe his interest was in Leslie, yet heard the story of Herbert Lossen. How he had been a strange child, always with that white face; how he had been clever beyond his years, arguing with grown men before he had been in his teens. How Mr. Nye – school-teachers, in the Toff's experience, were almost the only "misters" in the East End, except for clergymen of all denominations, most of whom were respected – how Mr. Nye had given him special lessons, how he had gone to a secondary school and then to Oxford. They were vague about Oxford, but they were sure enough that Lossen had been a "crool little beast", and equally sure that they had recognized him, a year before, when he had returned to Gay Street.

Yes, there was no doubt that it had been Lossen – there were surely no two people with the same pale face and the same queer-shaped eyes. It was the combination of the "Chinese" appearance and the pallor that made him conspicuous. They knew little except that he had stayed at Ma Parker's for a few days, during which time Les Parker and Lew Garney, who had been working in the Midlands for a long time, had returned. Les, Lew and Lossen, the three " 'ells" – the fat woman was convulsed at that joke – had been together a great deal. Then Lossen had gone off.

Was he well-to-do? If you asked them, he was well-oiled all right, *and* up to no good.

By degrees Rollison learned that they believed Mr. Nye was alive; he had gone to live in some out-of-the-way place, Harrow they thought, where the toff's school was. The school for toffs: at that there was more laughter.

By the time Rollison was back in the West End it was a

quarter to nine. He wanted to find more about Lossen, whose story had all the curious elements to attract him in itself alone, but he was more anxious about Jolly. The schoolmaster could wait until the morning.

Lett still sprawled in the easy chair.

"Any message at all?" Rollison asked almost before he had opened the door, and Lett shook his head.

"Nope. You're looking worked up, Rollison – don't tell me that something's really got you worried."

"I'm worried enough," said Rollison. "Walk towards Piccadilly, will you, and see if there's a grey Morris 1000 – OQX is the number – parked anywhere around."

"What *is* all this?" grumbled Lett.

He was a grumbler by nature, but actually went eagerly enough, for he knew that a case of importance was brewing, and he was one of many who believed that if he kept close enough to Rollison he would find a story that would hit the *Echo*'s front page. While he was gone, Rollison ate biscuits and cheese, for he had missed dinner for the second night in succession.

Lett's eyes were glowing when he returned.

"Yes, it's there."

"And the driver?"

"I'd say he's the man at the corner of the Terrace," said Lett.

"I'll slip down and get a look at him," said Rollison. "Then if you really want a job, you can come with me, but it might not be all honey. Jolly's been where I am going," he added bleakly, "and Jolly didn't come back on time."

"Count me in," Lett said briefly. "I suppose I daren't mention the police?"

"I'll tell you why not on the way," said Rollison.

He preceded Lett down the stairs, and caught a glimpse

109

of the Morris 1000 driver. He did not recognize the man, who stared past him as if disinterested, but hurried back to his car when Rollison climbed into the Frazer Nash. The Morris was behind him when he reached Piccadilly, and remained at a fair distance on the journey through Hammersmith, Chiswick, and the Great West Road. Nearing the end of the latter, and at the junction of the Bath and Staines Roads, the Morris stopped.

Rollison saw that in his driving-mirror, and braked abruptly. He saw that the Morris driver was going into a garage, and he fancied that it would take longer trying to reverse here and drive back than if he went to the garage on foot. The need for going to the garage struck him as being imperative.

"What on earth –" began Lett.

"Hurry," said Rollison, and he ran towards the garage, to the astonishment of passers-by, both motorists and pedestrians. Near the small office the driver, a man of medium height and dressed in light grey, was talking to a burly mechanic. Rollison entered the garage, and the shorter man's face lost some colour.

The mechanic growled at Rollison:

"What d'yer want?"

Lett was hovering in the background. The Morris driver, whose cap covered gingerish hair, edged towards the office door. The mechanic was aggresive, and in his right hand he held a spanner of sizable proportions.

"I spoke to you," he said roughly.

"And I heard you," said Rollison. He slid his wallet from his pocket. "I want a word with this fellow," he said, indicating the Morris driver. "I'll pay you a pound for the use of your office."

It was a chance that he had to take; the mechanic might be in the conspiracy, or might be no more than a casual acquaintance, unlikely to be loyal enough to push aside a pound note. Rollison slipped one from his wallet.

"Okay, mister." The man stretched out a grimy hand for the note, and then Lett shouted :

"Look out, Rollison!"

Rollison did not need the advice, for he was moving then, side-stepping a vicious blow from the spanner. He poked his elbow sharply into the mechanic's stomach with force enough to make the man gasp and lose his grip on the tool. The Morris driver made for the office, but stopped when Rollison said :

"This isn't a plaything."

'This' was an automatic, for he had not left the flat un-armed. He watched the man turn colour, saw the mechanic taking deep breaths, and was aware of the steady hum of traffic outside. If there were any interruptions before he had finished his interview it would mean a considerable delay. He did not want delay, but the garage was a busy one, and every moment he seemed to hear a car-engine slowing down outside.

Lett exclaimed sharply :

"Rollison, are you mad?"

"Block the doorway," said Rollison, and he motioned the mechanic towards the office and the Morris driver. The sight of the gun was enough to make them obey, and Lett filled the doorway, howbeit reluctantly.

"Get into the office," Rollison said to the others, and the mechanic stretched out a hand to turn the handle of the door. The door sagged open, and both men backed into it, with the Toff not two yards behind them.

Only then did he know that there was someone already in the office. It was shadowy, but he caught a glimpse of the blur of a pale face, and he knew that the man there was Lossen even before the harsh voice barked :

"Put that gun down, Rollison,' or I'll rip you right up. *Put it down!"*

CHAPTER FIFTEEN

7 Ledsham Road

IT was not a good moment.

Rollison saw the pale face as it disappeared into the shadows, so that he could not see the man clearly. He did not know whether the other had a gun, or what was likely to happen if he refused to obey. If there was a shooting it would attract attention outside, and he did not want the local police in yet; it would force a delay that he was desperately anxious to avoid.

But sharp reports often came from garages. He took a chance, and fired once. The crack of the shot merged with a frightened oath from the mechanic and a squeal from the Morris driver. There was no answering shot, for the two men backed into the office, preventing Lossen from seeing him. He went forward quickly, and inside he could see Lossen moving towards a second door.

He fired again.

He wanted to get the man's legs, but he failed. The door banged behind Lossen, and Rollison turned on his heel, heedless of the mechanic and the other man. Lett, his face a study in amazement, moved from the doorway. From the rear of the garage a car started up, and it appeared a moment later – a Bentley, being driven straight at Lett and Rollison. Lossen's pale face was livid, and his eyes were glittering; that he would have run them down was certain, but they jumped aside. The Bentley hurtled past them, over the pavement, and swung left, towards Staines.

Rollison snapped:

"Get in the Morris, and –"

He stopped abruptly, for a small Wolseley pulled up, with a policeman at the wheel and another already climbing from an open door. Rollison said in a flash.

"That Bentley, officer – it's my car. Can you catch the beggar?"

Perhaps his manner was the deciding factor; at any rate the officer went back into the Wolseley, which started off at speed, gonging its way past other traffic. Lett, breathing hard, watched it going in the wake of the Bentley. Rollison could see Lossen looking over his shoulder.

Very slowly Rollison took out his cigarette-case.

"Well, well, well," he said. "We get a lot of help from unexpected places, don't we?"

"You – you're crazy!" declared Lett. "You're absolutely asking for it, Rollison. When they find out that it isn't your car –"

"Don't be an ass," said Rollison. "Lossen was on the way to the house I want to visit, but he won't go near it with the police on his heels. If he dodges them, it will take him an hour or more to get to Ledsham Road."

"Did you say Lossen?"

"Yes – I was going to tell you more about it on the journey, wasn't I?" He lit his cigarette, and one for Lett. "Take it from me for the time being that our Morris driver came here to see Lossen – I thought probably to telephone him – and to tell him I was on the way to Staines. Also take it from me that Lossen is one of the more important pieces in this puzzle." He walked back towards the garage itself, but was not surprised to find that the mechanic and the other man had gone. He saw them hurrying down the road, but he did not go after them for they were headed away from Staines.

"Are you still in it?" he asked.

113

Lett exuded a long breath.

"I've *heard* enough about your tricks, I might as well see this one through. I will say you've the nerve of Old Harry." He gave the impression that his admiration was reluctant as they went back to the Frazer Nash. "Have you finished here?"

"I'd like to look round, but we can't do everything at once." Rollison climbed into his car, and started off. There was no sign of the police car or of the Bentley, and twenty minutes later they pulled into Ledsham Road.

It was not what he had expected.

True, the speed of events in the past hour had not given him time to brood much on possibilities, but he had not thought of the word 'road' used as loosely at it was in that part of Staines. The 'road' ran almost level with the Thames, some fifty yards from the bank. Small craft and one or two yachts were moored quite near the river-side. On the other were modest-looking bungalows, mostly of wood, and probably used for holidays.

Beyond these were three or four large houses, built for permanent occupation. Each was approached from Ledsham Road by a wide gravel path, uneven enough to send the Frazer Nash lurching from side to side. There were few people about, although a man was mooring a dingy to a landing-stage, outside one of the wooden bungalows. He took no interest at all in the Frazer Nash, and the Toff was not sorry.

The number '7' was painted in black on a gate-post of one of the houses. It was larger than an average suburban villa, and probably had eight or nine rooms. There was a detached garage, and an extensive and well-tended garden. It was set back from the other bigger houses, and about it there was something shadowy, an impression strengthened by a row of poplars, in full leaf, along the front of the garden.

114

The sun was gone, and dusk was about them, so that sounds were hushed even on the river, and it was impossible to distinguish objects at more than thirty or forty yards.

Rollison pulled up outside the gates.

Lett stretched his long legs, and muttered:

"This is a grim-looking place. What the devil *is* this all about, Rollison? It's past time you told me what to expect."

Rollison said slowly:

"I told you it would mean trouble, remember, Jolly's probably inside here, and he did not go in of his own free will." Deliberately he made no mention of 'Iris Brent' the first, but he was hopeful that he would find her there.

What mattered as much, just then, was the number of servants on the premises. He opened the gate and walked slowly towards the front door. Lett kept pace by his side, a little hesitantly. The dark, brooding shadows about the house, and the gloom which surrounded them, added an eerie touch. In broad daylight it would not have affected them; with the light fading it made them aware even of their own footsteps.

"What are you going to do?" Lett demanded.

"Knock, for a start," said Rollison.

He put the promise into effect as soon as he reached the front door. The rat-rat-tat echoed sharply about the garden, producing a hollow note, as from an empty building. No sound came, and he was reminded of the visit to Defoe's cottage, and the moment before he had first seen the girl.

Was she inside?

"There's no one in," muttered Lett.

"We'll soon put that right," said Rollison. "But we'll try again first." He banged more heavily on the door, and the echoes were loud in their ears before they faded. Then into the following silence came the sound of a footstep in-

115

side the house. Lett raised an eyebrow; he was getting on top of himself.

"That's one theory busted," he said. "If you thought of breaking in, you were crazy."

The door opened then.

An old man stood on the threshold. Not only was he old, but he looked in an advanced stage of senility. He had not shaved for some time. Watery eyes peered at them, toothless gums showed when he opened his mouth.

"Yeh, yeh? What you want, yeh?"

"Come on," said Rollison to Lett, and he stepped inside, gripping the old man's shoulder firmly but not painfully. The old man did not seem particularly surprised, but he kept saying 'yeh, yeh' in a querulous voice.

"Are you alone?" Rollison demanded.

"Yeh."

"You won't get any sense out of him," said Lett. "If you seriously think Jolly's in here, look through the place in a hurry, and let's get out."

"You're no more anxious than I am," said Rollison, "but Granfer is something of a problem. We can't hurt him, but he might be a crafty old buzzard." He put that to the test, releasing the old man and walking along the gloomy hall. As he went, the old one slipped with surprising speed into a room on the left, and at the same moment a sharp voice came from ahead of Rollison.

"That's far enough."

A man who made a vague silhouette against a glow of light coming from a room straight ahead, snapped the words. Rollison, confident that his movement could not be seen, slipped his automatic from his pocket. He could not see whether the other had a weapon.

He took another step forward.

"I told you to stop! I –"

116

What else the man would have said Rollison did not know. Lett had stepped to one side and pressed down an electric light switch. In the bright light which followed, Rollison saw the gun in the other's hand. He did not know that it was the man who had gagged 'his' Iris Brent. He did not know that the man was prepared to shoot, and that it mattered who touched the trigger first. He aimed for the legs, and he got his man, whose shot went towards the ceiling as he fell, his arms going upwards, the gun, after the first shot, slipping from his grasp.

"In for a pound, in for a ton," muttered Lett. He pushed the front door to, as he went into the room where the old man had hurried. Rollison heard him say: "Come on, Granfer, we don't want any more tricks from you."

Rollison bent over the man on the floor. Obscenities streamed from him, but stopped when Rollison threatened to punch his nose. The wound was not serious.

"Is there a small room here without windows?" Rollison demanded.

"Find out – ouch, I – yes, damn you! The next door right."

The 'ouch' followed a light tap on the nose, and in turn was followed by a brief inspection of the room on the right. It was little more than a clothes closet, but large enough to hold the wounded man and Granfer. Lett took the old man in, and Rollison lifted the other, whose name, he suspected, was Garney. The key was in the outside, and he turned it on them.

Lett was looking excited.

"Damn you, you're making me as bad as you are yourself. How many more do you expect to find?"

"Inside, none," said the Toff. "Our trouble is going to be in getting the job finished before Lossen or others arrive from the outside. We'll keep together, just in case of accidents," he added. "Jolly will probably be in an up-stairs room, but we'll look down here first."

The ground-floor rooms were empty.

They were well-furnished, in modern fashion, a factor which the Toff noticed automatically as he went through. The first search finished, he went up the stairs, with Lett only a step behind him. There was only one upper floor, but two short passages led from the landing. Six doors in all were in sight when they reached the landing, all tightly closed.

The first two were empty; the third was a bathroom. The next main room was locked, and Rollison used a skeleton key with a speed and precision which made Lett grimace. The room, however, was an empty bedroom.

Rollison felt his heart beating faster as he worked at the lock of the last room, after another blank. He could hear nothing except the pounding of the blood in his veins, and Lett's heavy breathing. The lock was more difficult than any of the others, and an appreciable time passed before it clicked back.

"Now," muttered Lett.

Rollison turned the handle and threw the door open. Semi-darkness greeted him, and utter silence. He groped for the switch in the room, pressed it down, and then as the light made him blink he muttered an imprecation.

For that room, too, was empty.

CHAPTER SIXTEEN

Discoveries

BOTH men looked about the bedroom, and then at each other. Lett's face held an expression lugubrious enough to make the Toff smile despite his disappointment.

"What a sell!" exclaimed the reporter. "I don't believe there's been any funny stuff in this place, Rollison. None of the rooms look as if they've been lived in for weeks."

Rollison resorted to a cigarette.

"If you care to ignore the old one and Garney –"

"Garney? How do you know his name?"

"I was told by a Mr. Parker," said Rollison. "I gather that Garney and Parker are old cronies who work for Lossen. The two men at the garage may make up the rest of this bunch. Parker gave me this address, and I've no reason to think that he lied. So – where is Jolly?"

"They must have moved him."

"That's taking the line of least resistance," said Rollison. "Because a thing isn't on the surface, one shouldn't give up hope. The answer is 'cellar' or 'attic' – what was the elevation of this place?"

"What the deuce are you talking about?"

"Elevations." Rollison was brisk again, the wave of disappointment receding. "The appearance of the house from the front, side or back, if you want it more plainly. A high roof or a low one – high-ish, wasn't it? There isn't likely to be a cellar. The place has been built in the last ten years or so, and cellars weren't put in post-war houses very often. Come on, we're looking for a loft."

119

"Don't you think we ought to draw the blinds?" Lett asked. "Anyone passing can see us."

"Please yourself," said Rollison. "I'm in a hurry."

The loft entrance – or what looked like it – was in the middle of the landing. Lett drew some curtains, Rollison took a bedroom chair so that he could reach the boards across the loft entrance. The boarded hole was larger than that of a loft in an ordinary small house, and when he began to push it up at one end, a whirring sounded loudly about the landing.

"Look out!" shouted Lett, who had just come from the bedroom.

Rollison ducked, lost his balance, and would have fallen had Lett not jumped forward to support him. Startled both by the reporter's warning and the whirring, Rollison stared up at the ceiling. The boarded flap had gone completely; from the dark hole which it disclosed a ladder was descending slowly. The glow from the light on the landing was just bright enough to enable them to see the pulley mechanism by which the ladder worked.

Rollison gave a brittle laugh.

"A mechanical loft-ladder, and it gave me the jitters! But it looks as if we're getting somewhere."

"They might have installed that just to store old junk."

"Yes, mightn't they? You stay by the ladder, and I'll have a look upstairs. You haven't a torch in your pocket, I suppose."

"No."

"All right, I'll manage." The ladder was firmly in position, and Rollison climbed up quickly. It would not have surprised him had an assault materialized from the darkness of the roof, but he put his head and shoulders through the hole, and nothing happened. There was ample room for him to get through, but before doing so he struck a match.

He found himself looking at a small landing – or what had all the appearances of a landing – and at plain wooden boards which apparently partitioned the roof. An electric switch was at his side, and he pressed it down.

A bright light made him blink.

"All right up there?" called Lett.

"Yes, stay put, will you?"

Rollison climbed through. The roof had been fitted with a floor as well as with the partitions, and when he was standing upright he saw a narrow passage, sloping on one side where it was built into the roof. The other wall was of plain wood, and there were two doors in it. Rollison went forward, tried one handle, failed to open the door, and called:

"Is anyone there?"

Into the silence which followed there came a voice which was positively excited.

"Mr. Rollison – *sir*!"

"Well, well, well!" said Rollison, and he beamed with great relief. "So that's where you've been hiding, Jolly! And they didn't think it worth while to gag you?"

"They – er – they did, sir." Jolly's voice was a little unsteady. "The door isn't very stable, I think – I think you could break it down."

"Why break?" asked the Toff.

He took a skeleton key, and in less than twenty seconds the lock clicked back. He stepped into a room which was brightened by the light behind him, but which had no light itself. In one corner Jolly was sitting on a stiff-backed chair. A scarf, or a large handkerchief, drooped from his chin, and he was sitting quite upright, in a position which must have been extremely uncomfortable. He was tied hand and foot to the chair, but was soon free, and trying to move his cramped arms and legs.

121

"Th-thank you, sir. I contrived to – to loosen the gag, but I felt it unwise to shout to attract attention until I had freed my limbs." Jolly paused. "Are you alone?"

"Mr. Lett is with me. Are *you* alone, Jolly?"

Jolly could give no satisfactory answer. He did not attempt to explain what had happened to him, but did say that he had heard people going to and fro in the loft, or attic-room. He had heard no woman's voice, but the harsh voice of a man whom he had heard called 'Lossen' had been used frequently.

"Yes, Lossen would be heard plenty," said Rollison. "Get down that ladder – you'll see it by the hole – while I look next door."

"I would prefer to assist you, sir."

"You'll have plenty of time for that later," said Rollison. "We might be in a hurry, and you won't be able to get down the stairs quickly." He wasted no time with the skeleton key over the second door, and the lock – a simple one, like all of those at 7 Ledsham Road – yielded without difficulty. His heart was beating fast when he threw the door open.

A small electric lamp was burning by a single bed.

On the bed, her face almost hidden by bandages, was a girl. He noticed three things in the first glance. She had kicked off her shoes, which were at the foot of the bed. Her ankles were tied. And she was wearing a costume like that of the girl he had seen at Defoe's cottage.

The bandages worried him; they did more than that, they frightened him, but he saw quickly that there was no need for his fears. They had been wound about her face to prevent her from shouting, and when he unwound them he saw her grey eyes looking into his with relief, but without fear; her eyes were red-rimmed and watering; her face was too deep a red.

"Don't try to talk," Rollison said quietly. "I'll have you

out of here in a couple of jiffs, and we can have the story later." He did not even moisten her lips with whisky from a flask, but untied her wrists – bound very tightly – and her ankles, pushed on her shoes and lifted her from the bed. He carried her without great effort to the loft ladder.

Jolly had just reached the floor below.

"Lett!" Rollison kept his voice low, but made the call sound urgent. "Take her, will you?"

Lett came forward, and stretched his arms upward. Jolly stood watching. Rollison lowered the girl into Lett's arms, and then went quickly down the ladder. The girl was swaying unsteadily on her feet.

"Can you carry her?" Rollison asked.

Lett picked her up. She said nothing, being too weak to think or speak. Lett led the way to the hall, Jolly followed and Rollison brought up the rear. There was urgency in his mind, for they had been more than an hour since leaving the garage, and he did not think Lossen would take long before reaching the house. If he had escaped the police, that was, and there was at least an even chance that he had.

Rollison opened the door.

"Get her in the car, and drive her to the flat, will you? You go with them, Jolly."

"But what of you, sir?"

"I'm going to have a quick look round," said Rollison. "Don't argue, man. I'll be all right. Get the girl safely away, that's your job."

Lett was already at the Frazer Nash. Rollison watched until Jolly had climbed into the front seat next to him and the girl had been put in the tonneau. As Lett pulled the self-starter, Rollison turned and went inside the house, closing the door quickly behind him.

Had he taken the easy course and gone with the others he might have missed a chance that would not be offered again. The house was his for the searching, and he went through the downstairs rooms quickly, going through all drawers and cupboards. He found nothing of any interest.

A clock in the dining-room ticked loudly, and he could hear it wherever he was. With the downstairs search completed, he hurried upstairs, but again he drew a blank. Not until then did he go to the closet where he had locked the old man and Garney – or the man he presumed to be Garney.

They were in exactly the same position in which he had left them, the old man sitting on a chair, Garney sitting against the wall, with his legs stretched straight in front of him. Hats and coats hung about them, and Garney was using one for a pillow.

"You're Garney?" Rollison said abruptly.

"Sup-supposing I am?" The man was truculent.

"That attitude isn't going to get you anywhere," Rollison said. "I've got Parker, and Parker was talkative."

The man let forth such a stream of obscenities that any doubt as to his identity – as Parker's 'friend' – vanished completely. But fear quickly replaced the outburst of anger, and he talked, but he could say very little. Lossen was not at the house often; Garney did not think there were any papers on the premises. He did not know any more than Parker did why Lossen had gone to see Defoe. But he corroborated Parker's story in such detail that Rollison had no doubt that he had the truth.

Garney maintained that he knew only of the house and the garage. He had no idea where Lossen lived himself – Lossen, he declared, was a crafty individual, who did not trust his hirelings more than he had to.

There was no further object in staying. Rollison wondered whether he could safely leave Garney and the old man in the house, and decided that neither of them offered any threat for the future. Garney would not be about for a week or more, and the affair would surely be over before a week was up.

He locked them in, and went to the door.

As he reached it, he saw the glow of headlights against the glass panels, and he knew in that moment that Lossen had returned. He did not have a moment's serious doubt of the identity of the driver of the car which was turning into the rough drive.

He hurried to the back of the house.

The kitchen door was locked on the outside. He used precious seconds working at it with his pick-lock and as, at last, it opened; he saw a shadowy figure before him. He slid his automatic from his pocket.

At the same time, footsteps hurried along the passage. He snapped:

"Stand aside, or –"

Had it not been for the darkness he would have escaped without too much difficulty, but the darkness worked against him, for he was clearly visible in the glow of light that came from the hall, whereas he could see nothing but vague shapes. Something hurtled through the air towards him, and caught him on the shoulder. It was heavy enough to make him lose his balance, although he kept his grip on the gun.

Whatever had hit him – a stone or a brick – thudded to the floor, and a second missile caught him a glancing blow on the knee. That stopped him from moving quickly, and when eventually he did turn he found himself looking into Lossen's face; even in the dim light its pallor was a noticeable thing.

So was the gun in Lossen's right hand.

"Put that gun down, Rollison." The harsh voice held a menacing note, and the now-familiar mixture of coarseness and culture. "I've told you what to do!" he added, and his own gun, already raised, moved forward an inch.

Rollison would have tried to shoot it out but for the men in the garden behind him. As it was, he knew that for the time being his position was helpless.

He let the gun fall to the floor.

CHAPTER SEVENTEEN

Talk with Lossen

THE falling of the gun was a signal for the two men who had approached the back door to push their way into the kitchen. They jostled Rollison forward, each man gripping an arm. They frog-marched him through the kitchen and the smaller passage towards the front of the house, and Lossen preceded them.

Rollison wasted no time in regretting that he had been five minutes – even three minutes – earlier. He had seen the risk and taken it. But he had been in worse plights, and he was not particularly worried. He was far more interested in meeting Lossen. There had been no chance before to talk to the man, to assess him properly except through the eyes of the Gay Street residents, whose gaze was certainly not impartial.

"Upstairs," Lossen ordered.

The two men – the mechanic and the Morris driver, Rollison saw by then – began to frog-march him up the stairs, but quite suddenly they found they could not move him. The mechanic swore.

"Come up, you . . ."

"I can walk on my own," said Rollison mildly.

"I'll walk you!"

"Stevens, go in front," said Lossen. "Swig, follow him."

Lossen stood aside while the others obeyed. Rollison shrugged his coat into a more comfortable position, and walked up the stairs between the two men. He did wonder whether they would try to get him to the attic rooms, but apparently there was not going to be any immediate climb up the loft-ladder. They took him into one of the bedrooms, and then stood on either side of the door while Lossen entered slowly.

The Toff, standing by the window – the curtains were drawn, thanks to Lett – saw the man properly for the first time.

The features, with their strange pallor and their Mongol or Chinese cast, were quite expressionless. There was no doubt that in his fashion Lossen was a handsome man, but it was in his grey-green eyes that Rollison found most to interest him. They were almost blank, and yet they glittered. In them was the soullessness – a word which actually sprang to his mind – of a cat. Steady, unblinking, unfathomable, but dangerous and forbidding.

The other men receded.

There might have been only Rollison and Lossen in the room, the others were ciphers, creatures who would spring to obey an order, but otherwise stand mute.

"Stevens, go and look upstairs," said Lossen.

"I shouldn't trouble," said Rollison easily. "The attics are empty."

Stevens hesitated. Lossen said, "Hurry."

Rollison shrugged as the man went out.

"Apparently I'm not believed. I –"

"Rollison" – Lossen had a habit of starting sentences with the name of the man he was addressing – "I want to talk to you, but not at the moment. Just keep quiet."

"It doesn't suit me," said Rollison.

"You'll make it suit you."

"We aren't agreeing at all well," said Rollison. "Must you behave like a stage villain?" There was a touch of irritation in his voice as Lossen raised the gun, which had never left his hand.

"I told you to be quiet."

"When the time comes for me to do what I'm told, I'll be out of this world for good," said Rollison. "Do you mind if I smoke?" He took his case from his pocket, and was intrigued to see that while the man called Swig started, Lossen made no sign that he was perturbed by the movement. The case had an automatic lighter built into it, and Rollison lit his cigarette. He pocketed the case, and said more evenly. "You're making a lot of mistakes, Lossen."

"How do you know my name?"

"Your name, most of your history, much of your reputation, and your habits as a child – I could give you a fair summary of them all."

He had the satisfaction of seeing that he had got past Lossen's guard. At that moment, however, Stevens came in to report that the attic was empty. Lossen turned his head.

"So."

"I did tell you," murmured Rollison.

"It was one of the last things you will do," said Lossen slowly. "I warned you yesterday not to interfere. You should have taken the warning."

Rollison leaned against the wall. The wood of a window frame was hard against the middle of his back.

"I was curious. I'm always curious. Lossen – you're making serious mistakes – I told you about that before."

"I made one when I left you alive."

Rollison laughed, and again it seemed as if he were genuinely amused.

"If I were to tell you the number of people who wished

128

they'd killed me when they first had the chance, you'd dis-believe me. And that wouldn't do." He was half-way through his cigarette, and he took it out and examined it critically. "One of the difficulties is that I don't do the thing I'm ex-pected to. Haven't you discovered that?"

"I –"

"No, let me get a word in edgeways," pleaded Rollison. "And let's get down to cases, Lossen. I came here with others, of course, and the others stayed outside after I'd got rid of the girl and Jolly. The moment they saw you arrive they were to send for the police."

"Don't lie to me," said Lossen dispassionately.

Rollison shrugged. "And you were reproaching me for not taking a warning. "However, the police will probably be half an hour, they're not likely to come on the strength of a 'phone message. They've had one wild-goose chase to-day – how did you manage to dodge 'em?"

Lossen made a quick, impatient gesture.

"Stevens – teach him not to talk."

Rollison saw the big mechanic come forward, and was only half-prepared for a blow on the chin which sent him reeling back against the wall. A second blow, delivered with all the force in the mechanic's hefty body, knocked him side-ways, and he had no chance to retaliate. Three punches to the stomach, delivered each time with vicious force, made him feel sick.

"That is enough," said Lossen.

Rollison was breathing very hard.

The callousness of the attack was not surprising; the way in which Lossen had ordered it was. It was obvious that the mechanic had acted on similar orders many times. Rolli-son's head was ringing and his stomach was queasy, but there was a fierce anger in him, although he knew that the others were using methods which he himself would be prepared to use if he really needed information.

Lossen moved forward.

He put his gun into a shoulder-holster, and brushed the hair back from his forehead. His eyes seemed to glitter, showing more green than grey.

"Rollison, what has interested you in this affair?"

Rollison drew a deep breath.

"You," he said.

"Are you just a fool?" demanded Lossen. "Do you want more of that treatment? Before I have finished with you you are going to tell me just what brought you into this business, and why you stayed in it. You are going to tell me where you have sent the girl, and you are going to tell me everything that you have discovered, or think you have discovered. If you don't start to talk immediately, Stevens will work on you more thoroughly."

Rollison said, "He won't be wise."

Lossen stepped back a pace.

"Stevens – go on with it," he ordered.

Rollison watched the big mechanic advancing.

Stevens gave the impression that he was eager to use violence, that he gloated over using it. Doubtless memory of what had happened at the garage encouraged him. There was a brutal expression on his heavy face, a glitter in small, porcine eyes. It seemed an age ago since Rollison had offered him a pound and had not been certain whether the garage was associated in any way with Lossen, or whether Swig had simply gone to use a telephone and send a warning message.

Rollison reasoned that he would be no worse off if he made a fight of it than if he took what was coming. He could see no further ahead than the next few seconds.

He backed against the wall.

"Keep still!" growled Stevens, and swung a wicked left

hook. His bunched hands were enormous, and there was no mark on them where he had previously hit the Toff. He went for the Toff's chin, and Rollison moved his head forward a foot.

Stevens hit the wall.

It was only a glancing blow, but it was received with such surprise and pain that he bellowed, losing control of himself for the vital moment that Rollison needed. He brought his knee up heavily into Stevens's groin, and the man uttered one long-drawn-out groan before staggering back.

The Toff went forward.

Stevens almost hid Lossen and Swig from him, although he could see Lossen's face. He pushed his hands, palm outwards, against Stevens's chest, and sent him staggering across the room, so that Lossen had to dodge swiftly out of the way. Swig was not so quick on his feet, and Stevens cannoned into him, then pinned him against the wall.

Lossen's hand was at his shoulder.

Rollison slid his cigarette-case out, a quick movement followed by another that was so fast that it would have passed for sleight-of-hand. He tossed it at Lossen, and it went straight towards the man's face. Lossen ducked. He did not go into a panic or lose his self-control. He just ducked from the case, which clattered against the wall, opening and showering cigarettes on the floor.

But the movement delayed the drawing of his gun.

Rollison made no attempt to reach him, but jumped over Stevens's legs and into the passage. As he reached the head of the stairs he heard a shot from behind him, the soft *zutt!* of a silenced automatic. The shot went wide. There was pain in his side, his head and his stomach, but he kept on, and half-way down the stairs vaulted over the banisters. He dropped to the passage alongside the stairs and was in the kitchen before Lossen was in the passage.

The back door was shut, but not locked.

Rollison pulled it open and plunged into the darkness. He turned left, and then kicked against a bucket which made a loud metallic clangour, and almost tripped him. He steadied himself, and went on, hearing the sound of footsteps from the house, but seeing nothing.

A shot winged after him.

There were no lights near by, although at a house two or three hundred yards away a blaze was coming from an uncurtained window. It gave him just enough light to see by, and he made for the road and the river-bank. He heard a second shot, knowing that the sound would not travel far. He reached the gate, which was open, and went through. Footsteps on the gravel seemed very loud in his ears. He plunged forward – and then without warning he found himself ankle deep in water. He could not stop his legs from moving, and the next step sent him forward in the Thames.

As he fell, he realized why it was: the tide had risen covering part of the road.

CHAPTER EIGHTEEN

High Tide

IT was not deep enough to swim in.

He could not turn back to the road, for he had no doubt that Lossen was waiting and watching, and he expected at any moment to see the beam of a torch shining across the water. He went forward, on his hands and knees. The mud of the river bed did not worry him, he was glad he had not found a shingle patch. Then he cracked his head against the side of a small dinghy he had seen moored near Ledsham Road.

Grasping the side of the boat, he waited until his head cleared. By then he was able to see in the light of the stars, and he saw the figure of a man standing on the bank, peering towards the murky waters. He imagined he saw a gun in the man's hand.

Slowly he waded round the dinghy, crouching as he did so.

It was bitterly cold in the water, and he shivered from head to foot – although that might have been as much from reaction as from the cold. Suddenly he lost his footing; the water grew much deeper, and when he had recovered he was standing almost shoulder deep. As he gasped for breath, he saw a flash of light from the bank, and from somewhere not far from his head he heard a bullet *plop!* into the water.

The sound of the shot carried more clearly on the river.

But the dinghy was between him and the bank, and gave him cover. He could raise his voice and shout for help, but there was at least a chance that no one would hear him, and certainly a risk that Lossen would get in a fatal shot before help arrived. So he dragged himself towards the mooring-rope of the dinghy, and with considerable effort took a knife from his pocket.

Opening the knife was not easy.

Cutting the stout rope was even more difficult, but he sawed it through at last, and the dinghy began to move on a swift tide which was lapping against Rollison's chin. He started to swim, with the end of the rope in one hand. No further shooting came from the bank.

He was glad that he had not to swim far, for he felt the weakness of his limbs, and a twinge or two of cramp scared him. But he was far enough out now to take a greater chance. He stopped swimming, clung to the edge of the dinghy and began to climb in.

Twice it almost fell on him. Laboriously he went to the

133

other side, so that when he put his weight against the dinghy the swift-flowing tide helped to keep it steady. Thus he was able to climb in. He groped for the oars, and found them. Satisfied by that, he rested for a while, letting the dinghy take him downstream.

The noises of the river were all about him.

The lapping of water at the boat's side, the call of a disturbed gull, the creaking of craft moored to buoys and presenting an ever-present danger, were about him. He saw lights on either side of him, some hanging from or attached to Staines Bridge; he was moving away from the bridge, and judged that he was at least a hundred yards from 7 Ledsham Road.

He peered towards the bank where he imagined the house to be. Suddenly the darkness there was pierced by head-lights, which moved first of all towards the river, and then turned right, towards the bridge and the main road. Rolli-son smiled grimly, and into the stillness of the night he said:

"They've evacuated Number Seven. I wonder if I ought to send the police there in a hurry?"

Then he smiled, less grimly, for there was no chance of doing anything in a hurry. He took the oars and began to pull towards the bank, finally reaching it half a mile or more below Staines Bridge. He was two hundred yards from a glow of light that came from a small house near the bank, and he walked slowly towards it, chilled through and shivering.

He reached the house at last, located the front door, and knocked. Then he waited, leaning against the porch, and wondering how quickly he could get to Gresham Terrace; for he was suddenly aware that the one fact which had emerged from the talk with Lossen was that the girl was extremely important.

Lossen might try to get her back from the flat – for he would surely know the Toff's address.

A middle-aged couple alone in the house, were at once helpful and anxious. He explained mendaciously that he had been mooring a dinghy which he had forgotten earlier, and had been caught by the tide. He was offered a change of clothes, given hot tea with a lacing of whisky, cigarettes and sandwiches; all of which he found excellent.

The good Samaritan, a tall, grey-haired, lean-bodied man, pulled at a short moustache.

"You're not the first to have trouble, sir – it's the highest tide of the summer – higher than most years, too. It rises swiftly here – you're not used to the river hereabouts?"

"I'm not a riverman at all," said Rollison, apologetically. He chattered for a few minutes but very soon he was at the telephone, speaking to Jolly.

Jolly sounded very relieved.

"Oh, yes, I'm fine," said the Toff, who made it sound as if he was apologizing for being late for an appointment. "But I don't know what time I can make it – I was fool enough to fall into the river."

"*Indeed*, sir," said Jolly.

"You're all waiting, I suppose?"

"Yes, sir, all three of us."

"I don't expect anyone else to arrive," said Rollison, "but you can never be sure."

"I quite understand, sir," said Jolly.

"Good. I'll get along as quickly as I can – I hope I won't be much more than an hour. Good-bye."

"Take great care of yourself," urged Jolly, and rang off.

The Toff smiled, turned, and then found his unexpected hosts looking at him fixedly. Then his eyes fell to the evening paper on the table, and he saw a photograph of himself; he

135

had been connected with the Defoe-Crossfield affair, of course – he should have expected that.

He raised one eyebrow, comically.

"We-ll!" exclaimed the Good Samaritan. "I hardly expected to see you in the flesh, Mr. Rollison! *Did* you fall into the river?"

"Literally," Rollison assured him. "True, I was in a hurry to get away from some acquaintances." Now that he could not avoid recognition, he saw a chance of taking advantage of it. He learned that he was still in Ledsham Road, that Number 7 was a house which was let furnished, and they knew of it because some friends of theirs had stayed there for the summer a year or two before. They knew nothing of the present tenants. They promised not to broadcast Rollison's visit, and even offered to lend him their car, kept in a wooden garage at the back of the house.

Rollison accepted that with alacrity and gratitude.

He drove towards London, warmer, much happier, regretful only that Lossen and the bunch at Number 7 had escaped. He turned over in his mind the wisdom of going to the police, and decided that before he made any official report he would see the girl at the flat. He had warned Jolly by inference that there might be trouble, and he was no longer worried that Lossen would make any effective attack.

Now that things were more normal, he thought it unlikely that Lossen would try, yet, at all events. Then his mind turned towards the puzzle, including the parts the Crossfields, Defoe and the girl had played in it. He thought that she was the most important cipher in the affair – provided she proved willing to talk.

Would she?

He put the fear that she might be obstinate aside, and drove past the garage where he had seen Lossen, with a smile partly inspired by memory of the police car which had unwittingly helped him. Then he settled down to driving through the nearly deserted streets of London.

It was one o'clock when he turned into Gresham Terrace. Only the street lamps were burning. Glouds now covered the stars, and a stiffer wind was blowing; he was glad that his immersion had not been two hours later. When he reached the front door of the flat he found that he had left his keys in his wet suit, and rang the bell.

He was a little afraid, even then, that something would have gone wrong; but Jolly, showing no signs of his own ordeal, opened the door, stood aside, and bowed.

"I am very glad to see you, sir."

"That goes for us both," said Rollison with feeling "How is she?"

"The young lady is sleeping, sir. She appeared to be very tired, very tired indeed, and so I suggested that she went into the spare room."

"Yes, indeed" said Rollison. "I'll have to wake her, but an hour or two's sleep will have done her good. What happened to you?" he added as he stepped into the lounge, where Lett was sprawled back in an easy chair, half-sleep. He raised one hand drowsily.

Jolly coughed.

"It was most unfortunate, sir. I reached the house – the somewhat peculiar nature of the road made it difficult to do so without being observed, or without revealing my interest in Number Seven, sir. Then a man who obviously recognized me approached, and pushed an automatic pistol into my ribs. I considered it wise to do what he suggested."

"It was wise all right," said Rollison dryly. "And then?"

"There was very little of moment, sir. I was bound and otherwise inconvenienced, as you doubtless perceived, and was like that when you arrived. I think that in another hour I *may* have contrived to obtain some degree of freedom, but

137

I was very relieved indeed when I heard you."

"I can believe that," admitted Rollison. "Well, Jolly – I can't remember being hungrier."

"I have prepared some sandwiches, sir – and I will make some coffee. Mr. Lett had his supper some time ago, and the young lady was hungry also. I suppose you are not yet ready to tell me what happened to you."

Rollison smiled, and leaned against the door of a spotless kitchen, telling Jolly what he wanted to be known. Lett hitched his chair up nearer to the door, so that he could also hear. He had been loyal, and had as yet made no attempt to telephone his paper, but he wanted a story through by two-thirty, to catch the late editions.

"That's reasonable," admitted Rollison as he ate sandwiches and reflected that he had had too few square meals in the past few days. "But let it be suggestive only – great events brewing – what has Rollison discovered? – you know the stuff."

"That's all very well," grumbled Lett, "but it ought to be meatier than that. Damn it all, I've seen you through a whirlwind of trouble."

"You can have all the meat tomorrow," said Rollison.

Lett raised one eyebrow higher than the other.

"So soon? Are you sure?"

"I'm going to be very disappointed if it's not over by then," Rollison said. "And you ought to get some sleep, you're going to be busy tomorrow, too. You're going to check up on Iris Brent's life history, how and when she met Crossfield, whether she knew Crossfield before she met Defoe. And you're also going to use your powers to find out whether Crossfield has a murky past. I won't be surprised to find that he has a number of skeletons in his cupboard."

"Who, Crossfield?" Lett was sceptical. "He's as straight as they come. Oh, he might have made an ass of himself

138

once or twice, but no more than that."

Rollison chuckled – and then stifled a yawn.

"I don't know much about Crossfield, but I think he's either up to monkey business, or else he's being blackmailed. He must have featured in the Press a lot in the past few years – and you're the man to get all the information collated. We don't want the police on it, yet at all events."

Lett shrugged, but as usual agreed.

"That's fine," said Rollison, stifling another yawn. "Now we'll see the girl – if I don't talk to her soon, I'll fall asleep while I'm asking questions."

"Why don't you leave her until the morning?"

"She's been left long enough already," said Rollison. "Did she have a bag with her? – I didn't notice one."

"No, sir," said Jolly.

"Well, let's go in. Or rather, I'll go in. You two can stand by the door." There was small chance of interrogating the girl without Lett hearing what was said, and he could hardly try to insist that Lett be kept out of it. He believed that he could rely on the reporter to keep any relevant facts to himself, and he stepped to the spare room.

"Don't wake our sleeping beauty too abruptly," said Lett.

Rollison smiled, widened the door, and then looked at the sleeping girl for fully twenty seconds before he went forward and touched her arm, lying over the eiderdown. She looked very lovely, but tired and pale.

She stirred at his touch; and then abruptly the telephone bell rang in the lounge. She stirred again, but did not wake, and the Toff waited while Jolly answered the call.

He was at the door a moment later.

"It's for you, sir – Dr. Whittaker, from Fern Cross."

Rollison stared.

"Whittaker, is it? At two o'clock in the morning? I hope

there hasn't been more funny stuff at the Hall." He slipped past Lett again, and the reporter pulled the door to a little, after a lingering glance at the sleeping girl.

Rollison said into the telephone:

"Hallo, there!"

"Oh, Rollison," Whittaker's voice was quite distinct; so was the anxiety which it held. "There's been a disquieting development down here, and I think you should know at once."

"Go on, please," said Rollison, and he thought of elfin Mary Crossfield; could anything have happened to her?

"I learned of it quite accidentally," said Whittaker as if deliberately drawing out the story. "I was called into Guildford for an urgent diagnosis – one of my patients at the hospital. Rollison, Defoe was taken away late tonight, no one knows who by. Kidnapped, I mean. The police are making inquiries now, but he seems to have disappeared into thin air."

CHAPTER NINETEEN

What's in a Name?

THE statement came with a shock of surprise which robbed Rollison of speech, and his expression put Jolly and Lett on tenterhooks to learn what had happened. At the other end of the wire Whittaker said:

"Did you hear me?"

"Er – yes, I heard. You're quite sure there could be no mistake?"

"Of course there's no mistake," said Whittaker testily. "He was in a private ward, and a policeman was actually in the room. Someone came in by the window, knocked the policeman out, and took Defoe away. They haven't been able to establish the time, yet, but it was probably about half past twelve."

"I – see," said Rollison slowly. "Don't take too much notice of me, I'm trying to acclimatize myself to this news. I haven't been mentioned in connection with the abduction, have I?"

"Great Scott, no! What on earth do you mean?"

"I have known the police get queer ideas about me," said Rollison. "I hope they don't this time, because I've been a long way from Guildford. Many thanks indeed for ringing, Doctor – I'll be down tomorrow."

"Tomorrow or today?" asked Whittaker, still somewhat testily.

"Eh? Oh, of course, today." Rollison said 'good-bye' and then rang down. He looked over his shoulder at Lett, shrugged, and smiled crookedly.

"Here's your story," he said. "Defoe's been spirited away from the hospital under the very eyes of the police."

"What!"

"It's true – I've a doctor's word for it."

"Jumping snakes!" said Lett, reduced to a school-level exclamation. "I – look here, I think I'll get over to the Street. They won't believe this if I telephone it. The doctor's name –"

"Whittaker, of Fern Cross, but don't print it."

"I'll need it for confirmation, that's all." Lett grabbed his hat and hurried out of the flat, while the Toff turned to find Jolly regarding him with a glimmer of amusement in his eyes.

"That is just what is wanted, sir. Miss – er – the young lady, may talk more freely now."

"Ye-es. But do you realize what a blow this must be for the police?"

141

Jolly pursed his lips.

"I was not *over*-impressed by the local Inspector, sir."

"I don't know that he deserves this," said Rollison. "Oh, well, one thing at a time. The girl – did you nearly give her a name just now?"

"I nearly said 'Miss Brent', sir, that is all."

"Well, what's in a name?" asked Rollison.

He wished that he were less tired, but he had to talk to the girl before the morning. If he let her sleep now, and slept himself, it might well prove a mistake which he would regret for a long time.

It was not easy to wake her. He called her three or four times, and patted her arm and then her cheeks, before she opened her eyes. She stared at him bemusedly, started suddenly, and tried to sit up abruptly. Of the fear which entered her mind then there was no doubt at all.

"It's all right," smiled Rollison. "We're both quite harmless." 'Both' was necessary, because Jolly was standing by his side with a cup of coffee. "You've had an hour or two's sleep, and I have to ask some urgent questions. Do you think you can manage to answer them?"

He was glad to see her fear subsiding.

She sat up – she was fully dressed but for her shoes, and Jolly had simply pulled an eiderdown up to her shoulders – but her hair was dishevelled. Drinking the coffee gratefully, she refused a cigarette.

"What is it *you* want to know?"

Rollison caught the emphasis on the 'you'.

"Eventually, what the others wanted from you," he said, "but before that, there are several small but important points. For instance, your real name. In case you don't remember" – he smiled at that – "I'm the man you lied to at least once near Defoe's cottage."

She put a hand to her forehead.

"Oh, I remember all right. I – I called myself Iris Brent, because – because it was the first name that came to my mind."

"Is that the only reason?" Rollison hoped that she did not intend to lie again.

"Ye-es."

Rollison sat on the edge of the bed.

"I hope it is, because too many things depend on what you tell me. You knew what had happened, you knew that Iris Brent might be suspected of attacking Defoe, yet you gave me her name. Was that the thing to do?"

The girl said : "She was there at the cottage, anyhow."

Rollison snapped : "When?"

"Just before I arrived. I thought that she had used the knife – I still think so!" She was a little defiant, and he was wondering whether it would after all have been wiser to wait until the morning, when she was fresher. "But it *was* the first name that came to my mind. Had I thought I wouldn't have used it. I couldn't think. Pat was –"

"Pat?"

"Yes, Pat Defoe."

"You know him well enough for Christian names?"

The girl stared at him for some seconds, and then she smiled a little wanly.

"Oh, yes," she said. "Husbands and wives usually do."

*

It was a long story.

It took two hours in the telling, and even then Rollison was afraid that there were factors which he did not know, and which Defoe's wife had not told him, because she could not recall everything at that time of night, and after her experience in the past few days.

She *was* Defoe's wife; and her Christian name was Moira. She had been married to Defoe for five years, and for the first two, she said, she had been extremely happy. Then things had gone wrong, as they often went wrong between young married couples. There had been quarrels and heated arguments, and then one day in a white-heat of temper he had left their house, and told her he would not come back.

He had not done so.

Moira Defoe began to tell Rollison all this with some hesitation, but once she had started, the words welled from her. He imagined that she had stemmed the truth up within her for years, and that for the first time for ages she was un-burdening herself. The relief of talking freely was so great that she spoke in detail of their quarrels, of the absurdity of them, and her own stubbornness when he had gone.

As she talked, he was thinking of Defoe's reputation as a wolf.

And, more importantly, of Defoe's 'engagement' to Iris Brent.

She went on:

"I thought it was hopeless, artists are always difficult to live with –"

"Who are?"

"Artists," she said a little wearily. "Sculptors if you prefer it. Pat did most of his work in plaster or in stone."

"There wasn't a studio at the cottage."

"Yes, there was," she said. "It's at the back of the garage – quite a big one. That was one of the troubles, he could never bear me to go into the studio, it didn't matter what was wanted or how urgent it was, I mustn't interrupt him at his work. Oh, that was reasonable, I suppose – but he would miss appointments, inconvenience a lot of people – arrange to go with me to a show and forget. He would forget everything, or say he had forgotten, except" – there was a bitter note in her voice – "his precious cricket. That was always first, he was never late for that."

Rollison said, "I've known men like that."

"Oh, I suppose he's not the only one. But the life *was* impossible – I knew that. And my people were against me going back to him, or trying to persuade him to come back to me. It wouldn't have mattered, if I hadn't been so *desperately* in love with him."

She said that very simply.

Rollison felt a great pity for the girl who spoke so slowly and with such sincerity. Defoe's 'engagement', his reputation – what hope did they hold out to his wife?

"I think I should have gone back," she said, "but then he met Iris Brent. We're not unlike. I suppose that attracted him at first. I was told that he was engaged to her. I don't know whether she knew that he was married. I do know it wasn't like Pat, and I couldn't really believe it. He might have been temperamental, but – well, women *didn't* attract him much. When I first knew him it was hard to understand. There were models in all degrees of undress about the studio, but I was never worried by that. He was quite impersonal towards them – I suppose you won't believe it, but it's true."

"Why shouldn't I believe it?" asked Rollison.

Defoe would have visitors, lady visitors, of course; models, about whose coming and going Defoe would not give a second thought. What was strange was the fact that Fern Cross apparently knew nothing of the studio; many things would be forgiven an artist, things for which an ordinary man would stand convicted.

Did Arnold Crossfield know?

Was there a simple explanation of the protracted tenancy?

She went on:

"People don't believe it, they don't understand the mind of a man who looks on beauty as beauty, not as something calculatingly provocative. I would have trusted Pat any-

145

where. I suppose living on his own worried him, and this Brent woman cropped up."

"You don't know how he met her?"

"No. Someone heard about the engagement, and I was told about it. I went to see him. He" – she drew a sharp breath – "he wasn't as kind as he might have been, but I suppose I went about it the wrong way. He didn't try to explain anything about her, but when I thought about it afterwards I – I had an impression that he could have explained her away."

She paused, and Rollison asked:

"What made you think so?"

She leaned forward a little, raised her knees, and clasped them, under the eiderdown.

"When you've lived with someone for a year or two, when you've been in love like Pat and I were, you do *feel* things that anyone else might laugh at. I'd told him that he was a beast to the other girl as well as to me, and said something about taking too much for granted, not trying to see beneath the surface. I don't remember clearly, but the thing got on my mind. I'd been unhappy with Pat, but I was ten times unhappier without him. I went abroad for a year, with my mother, and when I came back I heard that the engagement – engagement! – was broken. Then this horrible business about a breach case cropped up. I didn't know how Pat would get through it. After all, had the whole truth come out he would have looked an – an utter beast, and I wanted to – to try to help him. So I went, yesterday. I saw the girl coming away, and I went in immediately afterwards, in a flaming temper, until I saw him lying on the floor. I was frantic at first, then I saw that he wasn't badly hurt, that he would recover. So I stopped the bleeding, and then – well, I've told you what happened. The three men arrived, and

I went away. When they had gone, I went back. I just couldn't make myself go. Then – well, you came."

Into the following silence Rollison said :

"Yes. But why didn't you want to be seen? Why were you so anxious to keep your real identity away from me?"

CHAPTER TWENTY

More from Moira

MOIRA DEFOE told Rollison that she had not had time to think, that she had been at once frightened for herself, and for her husband. But there was more in it than that.

"I know he was doing something that – that he wanted kept secret. Please don't ask me to explain, I can't. But he had kept something from me during the last months we were together – that as much as anything else drove us apart. I was afraid that he was taking part in some kind of crime."

"Well?" asked Rollison.

"I didn't want to be connected with anything devious, especially something I didn't know about. I wanted to try to find more about it, before it was known that I was there. I'd stayed because I hoped he would regain consciousness, and talk. Then – well, I was just frightened, for myself. I had a passion-motive – don't they call it that?" she added bitterly – "for wanting to kill him. Who would believe that I hadn't? Who would believe me when I said Iris Brent was there before me? The scorned and neglected wife revenging herself on her husband, and getting the other girl involved! Can't you see everyone just *loving* that?"

Rollison did not know whether she had told him all the truth, but he did know that what she said was eminently reasonable. But there remained questions that he wanted answered, if she could answer them. He said:

"There are some other things, Moira Defoe. Your husband isn't well known, perhaps, but surely some people knew that he was married, and also learned about the engagement."

"They must have done."

"Even if he kept the affair with Iris Brent quiet for a long time, when the breach case started it was bound to come out."

"They couldn't be sure that he wasn't divorced. He'd kept away from people for a long time, I know. He had developed a passion for being on his own, almost a recluse. If I didn't know him better I would say that he was frightened."

Rollison said slowly:

"That could explain some of it. All right, there's another thing: I mentioned that I had come from Crossfield Hall. What made you look startled by that?"

She remembered the incident, for she answered promptly:

"I knew who Iris Brent worked for."

"Did you know anything else about her?"

"No, nothing that seemed significant."

"Who she worked for before, for instance?"

"No. I – Mr. Rollison, must you go on? Haven't I told you enough? I haven't talked so freely to anyone else for years!"

"And I appreciate it," said Rollison gravely. "I'm really grateful. And I think we can leave that for the time being. Let's take the story up from the time I was knocked out."

That was much easier. She told of the car ride, the arrival at the Staines house – she had not known where it was – and Lossen's assurance that she would not be injured if she 'behaved'. He had asked her for information about her husband, questions she could not answer.

"What kind of questions?" inquired Rollison.

"They thought Pat had some papers, and they wanted them."

"Did they mention what kind of papers?"

"No."

"Did they mention Iris Brent?"

"No."

"Do you know if a woman was at Staines at all?"

"If a woman –" She stopped, staring at him wide-eyed. "I didn't hear one. What do you mean? Was *she* there?"

"She knew what had happened to me and to you, she knew we'd talked, and she passed herself off as you, or tried to. Did you tell Lossen you'd given me her name?"

She was startled. "I'd forgotten – yes, I did."

"That's fine," said Rollison. "Lossen told Iris Brent exactly what to do, and she passed herself off as you. Quite a spot of double-dealing, but it didn't quite work out."

"Why on earth should she pretend she'd talked to you?"

Rollison smiled sombrely.

"There's a simple enough explanation of that. They wanted me to think that you didn't exist. They thought I could be tricked, and they even thought they'd tricked me, which is why Lossen was so annoyed at finding me near Staines. Why should they want to hide the fact that Pat Defoe's wife had been near the cottage?"

"It – it doesn't make sense."

"We can't have that," said Rollison. "It makes plenty of sense, we simply haven't seen how to read it yet. We will!" He stifled a yawn, and then fired three questions at her:

"Did you know the Crossfields?"

"No."

"Did Lossen ask you if you did?"

"No."

"Did he mention the family at all?"

"No."

"Oh, well," said Rollison. "I think we've done all we can for tonight, and you won't be sorry to get some more sleep. I wouldn't mind some myself. Is there anything you want?"

"No – no thanks." She watched him to the door, and then added: "Are you going to tell the police?"

"Not until we've talked about it more."

"Thank you," she said simply. "Good night."

"Good night, Moira Defoe." Rollison closed the door, and looked at Jolly, who admitted that he could not see the wood for trees.

They talked for ten minutes, and agreed that there appeared no urgent reason for advising the police of the presence here of Mrs. Patrick Defoe. A far more urgent matter was to find her husband. Had the story of Defoe's abduction from the hospital been told to the Toff at any other time he would have expected him to be with Lossen. Now he did not think Lossen had anything personally to do with it, and he thought, therefore, of Arnold Crossfield.

He wanted to learn much about that gentleman.

He slept until nine o'clock the next morning, when Jolly awakened him saying that Lett had called, and insisted on seeing him immediately. Lett came storming into the bedroom, weary-eyed, but apparently excited. He had got his story of Defoe's abduction in the *Echo*'s late London edition, and he had been congratulated by his Editor. He had also been given a free hand to follow the case to its conclusion. As a result he had been able to get others busy on checking the Crossfield–Brent association.

Iris Brent had worked for Crossfield for a year, but had known him for nearly ten years. Occasionally she had dined with him, occasionally lunched with him; as far as Lett was able to discover, there had been nothing beyond that.

"But," said Lett, while the Toff sipped tea, "there must have been some cogent reason. She's not the type he would philander with, even if he philandered at all, which isn't likely."

"Well?"

"Don't sit back there saying 'Well'!" snorted Lett. "This is your case, isn't it? All I can find out about her is that she spent some years in America – she picked up the accent all right, according to some of our chaps. She had a shot at the screen, but Hollywood didn't find her photogenic. We've dug up everything we can, of course, since the withdrawal of the breach case. She might have met Lossen in the States."

"How do you know he's been there?"

Lett grinned.

"*Now* you're on the right lines. Look at that."

'That' was a file of the *Echo* of seven years before, when Lossen had been charged in New York. It told of his acquittal, and also of his dismissal from the Crossfield Shipping Company.

"Well," demanded Lett triumphantly. "There's a Lossen–Crossfield tie-up for you!"

"Yes." Rollison frowned at the reporter. "But it's the wrong kind of tie-up. They should be at least bad friends. If Lossen was just getting his own back on the Crossfields, that would explain something, but not Arnold Crossfield's part in this. Iris and Lossen are acquainted – Iris and Arnold are old associates. I – Was she ever a private secretary before?"

"If she was, it's not on record. She's done some dancing and cabaret singing –"

"But now she's secretary to a man who thinks only of his business," said Rollison. "Whoever said that it didn't make sense was on the mark. I'd give a lot to talk with Defoe."

151

"You're not the only one," said Lett. "The Surrey police have consulted the Yard – I forgot to tell you that."

"I don't know that it makes a lot of difference," mused Rollison. "Did she stay at the Hall last night?"

"No." Lett had been through reports from the *Echo* man who had been watching the Guildford end of the case until that morning. "She came back to London."

"With Crossfield?"

"He stayed there."

"Where is she?"

"She has a flat – 81 Grant Mansions, Chelsea."

"*That* should be interesting," said Rollison, pushing back the bedclothes. "An early interview with Iris is clearly indicated. When it's over I'll tell you about the other girl, old man – there's no hurry for that, and it can keep for your tomorrow's edition. If I were you, I'd watch Crossfield."

"Are you putting something across me?" demanded Lett.

"I am not," said the Toff decisively. "I think this affair will end with Arnold Crossfield telling a very odd story indeed. We're in it from the wrong angle, as far as the mystery's concerned. There's big stuff at the back of it, my boy. But we were right on the mark for the personal angle, and that could be the more important."

"I wish you wouldn't talk in riddles," said Lett, irritably.

"I wish there were less riddles to talk about," declared the Toff. "And now I want my bath."

After he had bathed, Jolly dressed his head wound. Bandages were no longer required, but he could not wear a hat, for he had a wad of lint, fastened by adhesive plaster, on his temple. The exertions of the night before had not exactly helped his ribs, which Jolly massaged again with liniment.

"What are the instructions for the morning, sir?"

"Stay right here, and keep everyone out – strangers in particular. If there should be any sign of the Lossen crowd, ring the Yard, and ask for help. At all costs, keep Mrs. Defoe here – and if Lett comes back, don't tell him anything about the tragedy of marital errors."

"Very good, sir," said Jolly.

It was half past ten when Rollison entered Grant Mansions, and a few minutes afterwards that he knocked on the door of Number 81. He was prepared to find that Iris Brent had gone out, but he was lucky. She opened the door herself, and she started back in amazement when she saw him.

Rollison smiled, very charmingly.

"Hallo, Miss Brent! I'm lucky, then!"

She did not invite him in; he thought that she was frightened, and badly frightened. Certainly she had not expected to see him that morning.

"What – what do you want?"

"A talk," said the Toff.

"I – I'm just going to the office. I can't stay now!"

"Oh, come," said Rollison gently. "It's a necessary talk, Miss Brent. You did very well yesterday, and I had no objection to encouraging the police to think that we had met before, but you could hardly think I thought the same. Mrs. Defoe had told me quite a lot, you see – that both of you had been to the cottage about the time of the attack."

Every vestige of colour drained from her face.

"Mrs. – *Defoe*! You know about that –"

"Oh yes," said Rollison. "Hadn't I better come in?"

Dazedly, she stood aside.

He went in and closed the door, and stood looking down on her for some seconds. Then he gripped her shoulder.

"Who frightens you?" he demanded. "Lossen or Crossfield? Are they working together or apart? Why was young Crossfield shot, my precious? There are so many questions,

153

aren't there? And what about Defoe – have you any idea where he is?"

She raised one hand to her breast.

"I – I don't know what you're talking about." She spoke quickly and in a tone it was hardly possible to hear. "I don't know anything about it."

His grip on her shoulder tightened.

"Don't be a fool. Why did you make out that you had seen me? Whose idea was that – Crossfield's or Lossen's?"
He released her suddenly, and stepped towards a door leading from the small hall where they had been standing He saw terror in her eyes and she rushed from the front door to one on the left. As she reached it she realized her mistake, but Rollison knew why she was afraid, knew that something or someone was in that room, and she dared not let it be discovered. He went to it, and she flew at him. He had no easy task to ward her off, encircling her with his left arm before opening the door.

Half-carrying her, and with her fists still beating wildly at his face, he went inside. Patrick Defoe was lying on a single bed, adhesive plaster over his lips.

CHAPTER TWENTY-ONE

Part Solution

THE sight of the man lying there, staring wide-eyed at the door, created in Iris Brent an hysterical fury. She butted her head against the Toff's face, tried to get beneath his chin to jerk upwards, kicked and swore at him, the words coming in a low-pitched voice as if, despite her loss of control, she had enough sanity left to know that there must be no sound sufficiently loud to be heard outside.

Now that the door was open, and he had recovered from the surprise of seeing Defoe – the man's appearance there had been quite unexpected until the moment when Iris had been so anxious to prevent him from going into the room – the Toff was able to deal more effectively with the woman. But her strength was surprising, and she tried to knee him in the stomach. It was a false move, for Rollison slipped one arm beneath her knees, and was able to carry her towards an armchair near the bed. He forced her into it, and at last she began to raise her voice. Two shrieks were loud enough to reach the street outside, and Rollison wanted no interference then.

So he had to strike her.

He judged a jab to the chin carefully; her head went back, and her eyes rolled, her teeth clenched tightly. Her body relaxed, and she slumped back in the chair. He disliked that episode, but it did not worry him. He looked about him, saw a dressing-gown hanging behind a door, with a silken sash dangling from it. With the sash he tied her to the chair by the waist, making the knot behind the chair. She would come round in ten minutes or so, and he made sure that the blow had not been too severe before he turned to Defoe, asking:

"Can you hear me all right?"

Defoe nodded. He was pale, his eyes were bright and almost feverish, although Rollison did not think that he was suffering from a relapse.

"Good," said Rollison. "I'm going to get some gin or whisky and soak that stuff on your mouth before I pull it off." He went immediately to the small kitchen of the flat, put on a kettle, and found both whisky and gin. Next, he looked into the other rooms. There were three besides those in which he had already been. A lounge, a dining-room, and a double bedroom, obviously Iris Brent's. A glance in the wardrobe suggested that she lived there alone – he had

155

considered the possibility that Crossfield used the flat as a *pied-a-terre*, but there was no evidence of that.

By the time he had finished, the kettle was boiling. He poured water into a small bowl, found a sponge and a towel, cooled the water off by adding a little cold, and then rejoined Defoe. Iris was still unconscious. The gin was the more effective in making the adhesive on the plaster tacky, so that it pulled away easily. Rollison held a glass of tepid water to Defoe's lips, then washed his face, and finally looked at the bandages about the man's chest.

Not only were they in position, but they seemed to have been recently adjusted.

"Feeling better?" he asked, and Defoe nodded while he worked his sore mouth and his face muscles. One or two spasms of pain made him wince, but before Iris had come round he was able to croak:

"Who are you?"

"By name, Rollison," said the Toff. "I subbed for you in Thursday's match, and then started to look around with Wally Simm. The rest can wait, I hope – I'll give you a full list of bona-fides later. How have they treated you?"

"All right, apart from that blasted plaster! I could do with a cup of tea." Defoe moved a hand slightly over the coverlet of the bed, while Rollison went again to the kitchen, deciding that it would be better to get Defoe fairly comfortable before trying to get information. The woman was stirring when he returned a second time, and he fastened a handkerchief over her lips. Defoe was not able to lift the cup to his mouth, and Rollison sat on the edge of the bed, helping the man.

Defoe's voice grew stronger.

"Thanks a lot. What about a cigarette?"

The Toff gave him one, saying easily:

"There isn't a lot of time, and I'm going to take the

chance that you're fit enough to grasp the essentials. Before you talk, I shall – all right?"

"Go ahead."

Rollison told of what had happened at the cottage, of Moira's part in the puzzle, a little of Crossfield and of Iris, and something of Lossen. Defoe listened, smoking and showing no particular expression. When Rollison finished he said:

"And that's plenty, one way and the other! How – how is Moira?"

"She's all right, and I'm looking after her." Rollison was glad that the other's first question had been of his wife. He could not free his mind entirely of the way Moira had said: *"It wouldn't matter if I hadn't been so desperately in love with him."*

"Thanks," said Defoe. "Well, I can't tell you everything about it. I'll do what I can –"

"If I ask questions it might be easier."

"All right, try it."

"Who attacked you?"

Defoe turned his head towards Iris Brent, who was fully conscious then and staring wild-eyed towards the two men.

"That little vixen," he said. He spoke slowly, conscious of the need for conserving his strength. "The story goes back quite a bit. I've known her for some time, and we were pretty friendly. After – after the break with Moira I lost my head. Iris was one of my models – she's a good modern type, you know – and we strung along. She knew as well as I did that I was married, but I made a fool of myself and told her that when I was free we'd live together. I didn't stay in that frame of mind long – she had a string of other men, anyhow, and I was feeling pretty sick at messing things up with Moira. Is this clear enough?"

"It's fine," said Rollison.

157

"So I broke the association," said Defoe. "She didn't seem to mind very much, although she threw one of those fits of temper you've seen, but I was getting used to them. The next thing I did know was that she was suing me for breach. She swore that she didn't know I was a married man. The idea was simple enough – if I paid her a couple of thousand she would withdraw the action. If I didn't she'd go through with the case as far as she could, and make a nasty stink about it. It would give me a pretty unsavoury reputation, and of course she thought she was onto some easy money.

"And wasn't she?" asked Rollison.

Defoe smiled grimly.

"She was not! Incidentally, it was pretty generally understood among my friends that Moira and I were divorced, so the breach business didn't do more than raise a hum of scandal. Of course I could imagine it being a juicy bit for the Press, if it did get to the Courts, but as far as I could see it was going to be a case of who could bluff the longest. Iris withdrew the case, and she didn't get a penny from me. Not a penny more, I mean – I gave her a couple of hundred pounds when we broke off.

"A useful present," murmured Rollison.

"But not useful enough for her. Well, what else do you want to know?"

"Did she call at the cottage on Thursday and start threatening more trouble?"

"Yes. I told her she could do what she liked, and she picked up a knife and lunged at me. It gave me a turn!" Rollison concealed a smile at that understatement, while Defoe went on: "I don't remember anything else."

"You wouldn't," admitted Rollison. "But what do you know about Lossen?"

Defoe frowned.

"He came to see me once, and told me he wanted some papers which I had concerning the Crossfield companies." Defoe looked across at Iris Brent. "I don't think she should hear this, do you?"

"No," said Rollison. He wheeled the chair, Iris and all, into the hall, and shut the door on her. She glared at him when he turned away, but he felt that he could now afford to beam happily at Iris Brent.

"You don't lose much time," said Defoe slowly. "I don't know why I should tell you all this, but I'm taking you on trust – you seem to have given Moira a break, and I won't forget that easily. I was all kinds of a fool to – oh, well, that's over and done with." He paused. "It's a queer business, Rollison. I did some stationery – commercial stuff – for Arnold Crossfield three years ago. As a matter of fact, I met Iris through Crossfield. The commission took me to his house quite a bit, and without going into details I picked up some interesting items. Uncle Arnold wanted to get full control of the Crossfield companies, and he didn't want Bill to have any share in them."

Rollison stared, and said: *"What?"*

"It's true," said Defoe. "There was some talk of offering to buy Bill's interest. Well, I've known Bill Crossfield some time – he's a damn' fine cricketer! – and I knew he would be easily tricked into being paid off with a quarter of the real value of his share in the business. He's entitled, under his father's will, to forty-five per cent of the total shares."

"Yes?"

"Arnold was foolish enough to make some notes about it, and I lifted them," said Defoe with a twisted smile. "I must seem all kinds of an odd customer, Rollison, but I'm made that way. I just lifted them, and told Arnold that I proposed to hold them until Bill reached the age of inherit-

159

ance. I just left it at that. How Lossen came to hear of it I don't know."

"Iris and he are friends," said Rollison reflectively.

"*Are* they, now! That explains a lot we didn't know before. So she worked for Arnold and also tried to double-cross him – there isn't much that should attract me in Iris, is there? Well, that's about all I can tell you."

"It's plenty," admitted Rollison slowly. "But these papers – did Arnold commit himself very much?"

"Yes – they were notes he made and intended to destroy, I think. It gave the full value of Bill's share, and the amount he intended to offer for it. Nothing criminal, of course, but if they came to light they would blight Arnold Crossfield's wonderful reputation."

"Didn't it occur to you that it could be dangerous?"

Defoe shrugged.

"I didn't think much about it. I thought Arnold was check-mated, and Bill was all right, so I left it at that. Lossen came to see me in London – I've a studio in Chelsea – and he made me think about the papers for the first time for months. I had an idea I was followed down to the cottage that night, but I wasn't particularly worried. The papers are in my bank, you see."

Rollison smiled and rubbed his chin.

"Well, well, well! They even dug in your garden for them."

"*What's* that? Here, they haven't messed up the garden at the cottage?" Defoe showed a greater indignation at that possibility than in anything that had gone before, and Rollison drew a deep breath.

"You know, Defoe. I wouldn't be surprised if you aren't the oddest man I've met! Take it easy! They did no harm to the garden, so you needn't get worked up about that. There's nothing else you can tell me?"

160

"Absolutely nothing. Between you and me, I feel pretty well washed out."

"I'll get you to a nursing-home," promised Rollison. "I know just the place. I'll handle everything with the police, too, but if they come to see you before I turn up again, forget that Iris was here when you came round, will you?"

Defoe smiled. "All right, have it your own way. I – er – do you think Moira would care to look me up? Not the kind of thing a third party likes to dabble in, of course, but if you could persuade her I'd be no end grateful," he finished in some embarrassment.

Rollison said:

"She won't want much persuading, I fancy."

"She won't –" Defoe managed to hitch himself up on one elbow excitedly, and Rollison had to press him gently back to his pillows. "Good God, man, do you know what you're saying? She hates the very sight of me! I led her a dog's life, she –"

"Between you and me, she's in love with you," said Rollison. "Take it from me that she'll come."

"I – I can't believe that," said Defoe, but there was a brightness in his eyes which made the Toff feel very satisfied with one side of the Crossfield affair. But there were others which needed explaining, especially Lossen's part. The simplicity with which the Defoe problems had settled themselves suggested that the others would work out, too; he had told Lett that there was something big behind it all, and he had said himself that the human angle was perhaps the more important.

As far as the Defoe's were concerned, it was.

Rollison was in good spirits when he arranged with a nursing-home, whose principal had helped him before, to fetch Defoe – whom he called Smith – and to make no report to the police at least for the rest of the day. In view of the

161

publicity which the kidnapping would receive Defoe would soon be recognized, and Rollison could not hope to keep his identity quiet for more than eight or nine hours without damaging the nursing-home's reputation irretrievably. But he thought eight or nine hours would be enough.

By eleven o'clock Defoe was in an ambulance.

At five past, Rollison took Iris Brent into the lounge, keeping her fastened to the chair but removing the gag, and then he sat opposite her, lighting a cigarette and crossing his legs.

She muttered: "Well, what are you going to do?"

"When I know just why you attacked Defoe I can make up my mind. You may be the most detestable female in existence, but I doubt if you'd stick a knife into a man to get your own back – you'd be too scared of what might happen to you when you were caught. Who told you to do it?"

She set her lips stubbornly.

"I'm not in a hurry," said Rollison, "and if it comes to the point, the police can get the truth out of you. But it might save a great many people a lot of trouble if you talk to me. Including yourself," he added lightly. "It's for you to decide."

She said:

"I'm not saying anything to you or anyone! If you think they'll ever prove I did it, you're crazy."

"Defoe isn't dumb," said Rollison.

"He soon will be," she snarled at him. "How long do you think he'll be allowed to live?"

CHAPTER TWENTY-TWO

How Long?

ROLLISON regarded Iris Brent dispassionately.

He had not been careless when he had sent Defoe away. He knew the nursing-home well, and the nursing-home's male attendants also knew him. He had arranged for the ward to be watched constantly, and he had made sure that the ambulance had not been followed. He did not think there was much danger to Defoe, and yet the woman seemed quite certain of what she said.

Did she think the danger was from Lossen's men?

Or was she thinking of Crossfield?

He had assessed her reasonably well at their first meeting. She was hard, brazen, and money-loving. She would reckon everything in terms of pounds, shillings and pence, and there was no such thing as real affection in her make-up. It was almost a sacrilege that she should be outwardly so much like Moira Defoe.

But the operative word describing her was "hard".

She had proved how long she could carry a bluff in the breach case, and he did not think she would talk easily. The possibility of a trial and of being convicted for the assault on Defoe, which would surely be listed as attempted murder, did not frighten her. The fear she had shown when he had first arrived had quite gone, so that she must be confident that she could evade danger. To make her talk he had to break that confidence; since he did not know what caused it, that was not going to be easy, even if it were possible.

There were other things.

That Arnold Crossfield had planned to cheat Bill out of his rightful inheritance was easily understandable; there was no reason why Rollison should not believe what Defoe had told him about that. Crossfield's calm acceptance of the injury to Bill was explained to some degree – he cared nothing what happened to his nephew. Moreover, Crossfield's attitude towards the youngster seemed as clear as day, by then; he wanted to drive Bill out of the Crossfield Combine, and he chose a way of doing it which at least showed a psychological insight into the workings of the youngster's mind. Bill would have been ready to accept any settlement, and as easily persuaded that it was a fair one.

But – was that all?

Why had Parker shot Bill, at Lossen's order?

Why did Lossen want Bill out of the way?

Why had Lossen gone for the papers which Defoe had taken?

That Iris knew of the papers, through Crossfield, and had passed word of them on to Lossen was beyond reasonable doubt, but Lossen's part still had to be explained.

There was one obvious explanation: Lossen had a substantial grudge against the Crossfields, and with those papers would be able to victimize Arnold, who would surely be prepared to pay heavily to prevent the notes being published, or even spread about surreptitiously. There could be more in it than that: Rollison was fully aware of the fact that there might be others behind Lossen, that he had seen only the effects of the conspiracy, and knew nothing of the deeper motives, except as far as Iris and Crossfield were concerned. Defoe's part was reasonably explained, and if he found why Iris had attacked her late "fiancé" he might be well on the road to explaining Lossen's motives.

There was a silence for some minutes after she had said: "How long do you think he'll be allowed to live?" and then Rollison stood up abruptly, and stepped towards the window.

164

"He'll live to a ripe old age, my sweet. Don't get a fool idea in your head that anything else will go wrong with Defoe. I asked you before – who told you to knife him? Crossfield or Lossen?"

She spat: "Find out!"

"That's precisely what I propose to do," said Rollison. He stepped towards a telephone and lifted it.

"What are you going to do?" He had succeeded in making her anxious.

"I'm going to ring Arnold Crossfield, tell him you're here, tell him that you've been working with Lossen and passing on information which you've wheedled from your sugar-daddy. Once he knows that he won't think so well of you."

She gasped: "You – you mustn't tell him that!"

"Why not?" asked Rollison coldly.

"No, you mustn't, he – Rollison, he's going to marry me! That's why I withdrew the case, he didn't want to be mixed up in any scandal! That's why he gave me an alibi for Thursday – he knows I hurt Defoe, but he's protected me!"

Rollison said slowly:

"I thought he had. And so you're a couple of lovebirds, are you?"

"Don't talk like that! I didn't think he would ever talk of marrying me, that's why I helped Lossen! I didn't tell Lossen much, only about the papers that Defoe had taken, that's all! They can't say I knifed Defoe if Arnold says I was with him until the late afternoon, they can't do it! They'll say Defoe got confused, they'll look for –"

She stopped abruptly, and Rollison said coldly:

"They'll look for his wife, won't they? And you know that she was there. So Lossen was holding her until the moment came for handing her over to the police." His voice

165

was low-pitched and bitterly contemptuous. "I'm beginning to see very clearly now."

"I – I didn't think of his wife! "

"You didn't think enough before you started talking,"
said Rollison. "My Lord! What a mix-up! Crossfield wants
to marry you. Lossen wants something on him. Crossfield
gives you an alibi. Lossen knows it's faked, holds Moira
Defoe – the victim you've got ready for the stabbing charge
– and will only release her for the police when Crossfield's
done what he wants him to do. That's the lot, isn't it?"

"I – I don't know! "

"I'll go through it again, in reverse. Lossen wants to get
a blackmail hold on Crossfield. He can't get the papers, but
once Crossfield has sworn an alibi for you, Lossen can break
it unless Crossfield does as he's told. You're helping Lossen
to do that. Once he's got the hold, and once you're married
to Crossfield, you and Lossen have him just where you want
him." He paused for a moment, hardly able to realize that
he had seen the whole of the conspiracy, hardly able to
appreciate the full subtelty of it. Then: *"Why does Lossen
want that hold?"*

"I – I don't know! "

"Don't play the fool," said Rollison roughly. "I can put
the whole case to the police and fit in all the details, except
the answer to that question. I can even tell you why Bill was
shot. *Lossen proposed to pin that on to Crossfield.* Parker
and Garney would have sworn they had their orders from
Crossfield – that's so, isn't it?"

"I – oh, dear God! Yes. That's true, everything was
worked to put Crossfield in Lossen's power, there was
nothing else! I started the breach case to get money, but
then I thought I could make Defoe give me those papers for
Lossen. It's the truth, I tell you! I knew on Thursday that
he wouldn't do a thing about it, I lost my head, I didn't

have anyone's orders to attack him. You must believe that; I didn't know what I was doing! Then I saw what I'd done. I just lost my head and ran away. I met Lossen, and he had been watching, he knew Defoe's wife had been near. He – he told me he would look after everything."

She stopped, breathing very hard, her lips drawn back over her teeth. There was nothing nice to look at about her.

Rollison said slowly:

"So that's all of it, except Lossen's part."

"Yes, it's everything! Rollison, let me go away – I won't let them blame Moira, I'll leave the country, I'll do anything!" She was gasping every word, and her eyes were staring. He had utterly unnerved her, and she was close to breaking down completely. He was pondering the complications of the affair, and its simple foundation – Lossen's desire to get a stranglehold on Crossfield. The other things were incidental.

The question now was – how could he make Lossen talk?

Could Iris Brent help?

He had no thought of letting her go, or giving her a chance to escape the police. It was a question purely of judging the right moment for handing her over to the authorities, for once free she would twist round again, and would try to implicate Defoe's wife, perhaps bringing tragedy into a life which had already known more than its fair share of trouble.

She gasped:

"What are you going to do?"

Rollison said: "Where can I find Lossen?"

"I – I don't know."

"Haven't you lied enough?" snapped Rollison. "Where can I find him?"

"He – he had a house in Staines –"

"I know all about that, but he didn't live there. Where does he live?"

She breathed very heavily, her breast rising and falling, her hair dishevelled. She strained against the sash at her waist, as if in supplication, but he stood hard-eyed in front of her.

Then:

"If I tell you, don't let him know where you got it from. He'll kill me, he's deadly. Rollison, promise me that, I'll do anything if you'll keep Lossen away from me!"

"I won't tell him," promised Rollison.

She was silent for a moment, except for the harshness of her breathing, and then she said:

"He's got a house in Chelsea – Bank Street, Chelsea."

"The number?"

"Twenty-five. Only I know that he lives there, he goes by the name of Sanderson, he –"

"Sanderson, of 25 Bank Street, Chelsea," said Rollison. "That should be good enough, *if* you've not lied." He lit a cigarette. "I'm going to leave you here, just as you are. I shall have the mansions watched, so you can't get away." He stepped to a telephone, and it was in his mind to ring a certain gymnasium in the Mile End Road, where a Cockney friend ran a flourishing boxing business, promoting small fights and, as a welcome side-line, sending out men to help the Toff when help was wanted. Men would be at the mansions within half an hour, and half an hour should make no difference to his visit to Lossen.

He lifted the instrument.

Then he heard a sharp *click* at the door, and he swung round. But he was too late to do anything, too late to get at his automatic, for another gun showed at the door, covering him. He kept the telephone in his hand, and the gun by the door spoke – a sharp, familiar sneezing sound. The telephone broke into a hundred pieces, but Rollison's hand was untouched.

168

Lossen entered the room, and said:

"Move away, Rollison. Well, you little bitch, you gave me away, did you?"

CHAPTER TWENTY-THREE

Showdown

ROLLISON'S wrist was stinging from the wrench of the telephone being shot from his hand.

Iris Brent's lips opened, and she tried to scream, but no sound came from her lips.

Lossen moved his gun towards her.

Rollison said: "Lossen, don't –"

"Shut up," said Lossen in a low-pitched voice, and he squeezed the trigger twice. One bullet entered the woman's forehead, plumb in the centre; another went into her chest, on the left side. The scream turned into a choking gurgle, which ended in a rattle at the back of her throat. The small hole in her forehead grew larger as blood welled from it. She slumped forward in her chair, motionless.

Lossen turned to the Toff.

"Rollison, I've been hearing things about you," he said. "You think you're so hot that you burn. I'll hot you up all right."

Rollison said nothing.

"Lost your tongue?" Lossen said in the cold harsh voice. "It's too late to help you. You talked too much yesterday, Rollison, and the kind of luck you had won't come twice. You worked it all out so well, it's just too bad that you can't yelp to the police."

Rollison said with an effort: "I don't like the word 'yelp'."

169

"I don't give a damn what word you like – shut your mouth! You got down to it all, Rollison, you worked on Iris so that she cracked – sure, I'll give you that. But you don't know what I'm after, do you? I'm going to smash Crossfield until there isn't a Crossfield company left except in little pieces. You want to know it all – all right, you can have it. I was hired to find something on Crossfield so that competitors could quieten him down. Who hired me doesn't signify. When I saw I could get the gen on him and get paid for it, that was fine. Only *I* was going to use it – understand me? People don't throw me out on my neck without wishing they'd changed their minds. *And* they don't act the way you did. Well, you know it all now," he rasped. "Now what are you going to do with it?"

Rollison said: "I haven't had time to consider."

Lossen stared at him, and then a smile twisted his lips.

"You've got some nerve," he said. "I'll grant you that. But I can tell you what you're going to do with it, you needn't do any thinking. You're going to take it to your coffin – the dead can't talk."

"It's pleasant to hear you coin a phrase," said Rollison.

"What's that?" Lossen frowned, and then the irony sank in, and the twisted smile showed again. "Yes, you've got some nerve," he said. "It won't last any longer than you. I listened-in to all you told Iris, and there's just one thing you can tell *me*. Where are Defoe and his wife?"

Rollison said: "Don't you know?"

"Give it me straight, Rollison. I don't want to know so badly that I won't shoot you before I find out. Only there are places I can shoot and make it easy, like I shot Iris. That was merciful, Rollison. Stomach wounds aren't."

"I've always had an excellent stomach," said Rollison.

"What are you giving me?" rasped Lossen.

Rollison actually laughed.

He did not feel at all like laughing, because he was quite prepared to believe that he would not get out of the flat alive. The quality of murder in Lossen wanted no further demonstration, and it seemed as if the issue was simply one between a painful death and a quick one. Had he been able to get through to the gymnasium before this, there could have been a chance. He did not see one then, and he set his attitude on the basis that he might prolong the interview, and give the Fates a chance to enlist on his side, although he did not think that was likely.

The laughter puzzled Lossen.

"Rollison, what's funny?"

"Life, and your share in it," said Rollison, easily enough. "I didn't really do you justice, did I? I thought you would be easy, but –" He shrugged. "I suppose I'm allowed a final cigarette?"

"You're allowed nothing – keep your hands away from your pocket!"

"You still have my case, anyhow," said the Toff regretfully. "Unless you left it at the Staines house. All right, get it over."

"I asked you a question."

"I don't propose to answer it."

"Refusing won't help you."

"It will help the Defoes."

"Don't you believe it! The most it will do is to prolong their lives for a few hours, that's all. I'm no fool, and I've planned this for a long time. Defoe held out against me – folk who do that get paid, the same as Iris was paid, the double-crossing little bitch. If I can't smash Crossfield I'll kill him, I'll make a thorough job of it and then fade out. You won't stop anything by holding out on me, but you'll make it easier for yourself."

Rollison pursed his lips.

"We-ell, if you put it like that –"

"That's better. Make it fast."

"I'm not in such a hurry as you," said Rollison. "Defoe has gone to the South of France for his health, and his wife is taking a round-the-world trip before joining him. If you have your way I'm going for a longer journey, but that might be as imaginary as the Defoes'."

He glanced at the window. The flat was on the third floor, and a jump through the window held out no hope of escape, although it would create an alarm at the mansions, and Lossen might be held for questioning. He thought of a crowd about Lossen, and the man's gun. He would try to shoot a way out, of course.

Why didn't he shoot now?

Lossen said viciously:

"Rollison, you don't know what you're doing. I'll make you scream for the mercy of death!"

"Are you acquainted with hell?" inquired Rollison.

He saw the slight upward movement of Lossen's gun, and was prepared then for the shot. He tensed himself for a sideways leap, although he did not think there was any chance of doing more than causing a fractional delay.

But he was wrong.

They did not hear the front door of the flat open, but they did hear a man's voice call:

"Iris – are you in?"

Lossen half-turned his head, and Rollison jumped. He saw the spurt of flame from the automatic, and he felt the sharp pain as a bullet entered his shoulder, but its impact was not square enough to stop him, and Lossen had no time for a second shot. Rollison thudded into him, crowding a desperate forward punch from the man, and then the force of his leap carried them against the wall.

His left arm was quite useless.

172

Lossen punched at his face and sent his head jerking back, while from the hall came the man's voice again; it was Arnold Crossfield, and there was alarm in his voice where there had been testiness before.

"Iris! Where are you?"

Rollison squeezed his arm between the wall and Lossen's neck, and then doubled it. He caught the man's neck in a tight hold which made Lossen gasp, but Lossen still held his gun, although he could not bring it into position for firing. They were making little noise then, except that of heavy breathing. Their faces were within two inches of each other's, Rollison's red, Lossen's very pale.

Footsteps came outside.

"Iris –"

Rollison had Lossen's left hand about his throat, and the pressure stopping him from speaking. He forced the man's right arm against the wall, trying to prevent him from raising his gun. From outside there was silence; inside the breathing of both men was choked and laboured.

Crossfield opened the door.

The first thing he saw was Iris, slumped forward in the chair. He uttered a sharp cry, stepped forward, and then saw the others. Rollison could just see him, out of the corner of his eye. Crossfield stood quite still, staring. He seemed to be there an age, and the Toff's mind was forming words which his lips could not utter. He felt Lossen raising his gun-arm, slowly but relentlessly, and the pressure at his own neck increased. He could not make his grip any tighter, but he pressed with all his weight against the man, pinning him to the wall. It would not have been so bad had his left arm been any use at all. The numbness had gone from it, and it was beginning to ache.

If only Crossfield would move . . .

Then Crossfield did; *towards the door.*

There was little doubt of what was in his mind; he wanted to get away, to fly from danger. He saw two men in a life-and-death struggle, and his own safety mattered more than anything he could do for either of them.

Rollison croaked:

"Crossfield, come –"

The man went out, leaving the door open. Lossen twisted and pressed Rollison's injured shoulder against the wall, so that the pain was excrutiating. Rollison could hardly move, barely maintain his own pressure. Sweat was running down his forehead and his cheeks. He thought he saw a twisted smile on Lossen's lips as if the man realized that he was winning, and that it was a matter only of minutes before he got through.

Rollison thought: "If I can reach the door and close it. If I can reach the door –"

There was a chance, now that he had no need to open it. He relaxed his pressure a little, on everything except Lossen's gun-arm, and strained his head away. Lossen's fingers bit into his flesh, the breath was choked from him. Then he wrenched, at the same moment releasing Lossen. The two movements succeeded where one at a time would have failed.

For a split second he was free.

He lurched for the door, no more than four feet away from him, but his head was swimming, and his knees were weak. He reached it. He saw Lossen still leaning against the wall, unable to get full control of his muscles. The man raised his gun-arm very slowly; the cramp in it prevented him moving more quickly.

Rollison reached the hall.

But closing the door was a different matter. His fingers were numbed, lifeless. He touched the handle but could not feel it, and the door did not move. It opened into the hall, so he could not close it by leaning against it.

He stopped trying.

He turned towards the front door, which was closed. He staggered a few yards towards the room where he had found Defoe. On the opposite side of the hall he caught a glimpse of Crossfield, searching a dressing-table. He thought there were papers in Crossfield's hands, but could not be sure.

He saw Lossen coming unsteadily from the other room, but the man's arm was raised. He fired, and Rollison felt something tug at the back of his coat. He half-fell into the small bedroom, went behind the door, and managed to close it. As he did so he felt a pressure from the other side.

He dragged a chair and managed to jam it beneath the handle. He had never been so weak, so sick, so useless. He leaned against the wall behind the door, and then heard a shot, louder than any others; the silencer was off the gun. He heard the splintering of wood, and saw a hole leap into the panel of the door.

Lossen was trying to get him through the wood.

The door creaked under a kick or a lunge, quivered, and opened an inch or more. The chair would not hold it under heavy pressure, and Lossen had regained some of his strength; he had no wound, he had not spent himself in the past three days as the Toff had done.

The window seemed a mile away.

Rollison kept quite still, taking in deep breaths of air. A second shot came through the panel, and the door opened another two or three inches. Lossen began to try to squeeze through. Rollison raised his sound arm, and the muscles were no longer cramped and quite useless, but it seemed an age before he was able to get to his pocket for his own automatic.

But it was in his hand at last.

Lossen, unaware of that, made a final effort and came

175

into the room, staggering with the weight of his rush. Rollison touched the trigger of his gun then, and although the bullet was wide of its mark – Lossen's shoulder – it went through the top of his arm. The shock made the man drop his gun. Lossen half turned, but Rollison fired again.

He hit Lossen in the leg.

Lossen pitched forward as the roar of the shot echoed through the small flat. Rollison stood swaying by the open door, and saw Crossfield coming from the room opposite. The old man's face was not good to see, but he stopped when he saw the gun.

"Put – put that away!"

Rollison drew a deep breath.

"Not yet," he croaked. "This is – a final showdown. The one and only." He hardly knew what he was saying, and wondered if he could hold the gun up long enough to stop Crossfield from going. He wanted to do so many things. He wanted to make Crossfield talk, he wanted the police, he wanted to be sure the Defoes were all right, he wanted . . .

He forgot what he wanted.

Crossfield stood staring, Rollison swayed but kept his gun fairly steady, and then a key scraped against the front-door lock. The sound was very loud in the flat, because of the tension. Rollison's mind began to work again as he wondered who else had a key. Defoe had said the woman had a string of men-friends, it might be one of them, it might be anyone.

The door opened, and a woman gasped:

"Oh!"

Rollison went two steps forward, into the hall. Crossfield backed into the bedroom; he *was* holding papers. But for the moment Rollison was less interested in him than in the woman or girl who was standing by the open front door.

It was hard to believe.

It was like a delusion, and he actually wondered if the strain was making his eyes play tricks. An absurd thought, but surely not so absurd as the fact that Mary Crossfield was standing there and staring.

Mary Crossfield had a key to Iris Brent's flat!

CHAPTER TWENTY-FOUR

Whole Solution

SHE was so tiny.

Elfin and pretty, an ethereal creature, who surely knew nothing of this business; yet she had that key. Rollison turned towards her, and the gun turned also. She was standing quite still, and the colour had drained from her face.

"Rolly —"

"Come – in," gasped Rollison.

Then she turned away.

He was so surprised that he did not touch the trigger of his gun. It did not occur to him that she would be scared of the sight of him, that he was a frightening apparition. He heard Crossfield say something which was barely audible, and then he heard heavy footsteps, a man's voice outside saying:

"What's happening?"

It was hazy, then. He saw a policeman's uniform, and a man in shirt-sleeves; the porter of the flat, although he did not learn until afterwards that the man had heard the shooting when the silencers from the two guns had been taken from service, and had summoned the police immediately – the police being represented by a constable who had been outside. The man in blue had a hand on Mary

Crossfield's arm. The girl was looking frightened.

Stolidly, the law advanced.

"Put that gun down," the man said, and afterwards Rollison appreciated the courage of it, although the constable probably had no thought of bravery. Rollison lowered the gun, and then leaned against the wall; without its support he would have fallen.

Then he saw Crossfield come forward, and through a haze he heard the man say:

"Arrest that man, officer! He's gone berserk – he's killed a woman, and tried to kill me!"

*

Why should the policeman disbelieve it?

Rollison knew that there was no reason, knew also that Crossfield wanted only to gain time. Why, he did not know. Crossfield wanted the Toff away and under escort, wanted an opportunity to get away himself. Surely not to run, or to flee the country?

Wearily, Rollison eyed him.

The papers were out of sight, and Crossfield was in complete control of himself. The policeman released Mary, and stepped to the Toff.

"Don't try anything," he warned.

Rollison muttered:

"Not me, officer. He's trying it –"

"I tell you he tried to kill me!" snapped Crossfield, and then he started to pour out a spate of words which could have only one meaning – to prevent the Toff from speaking. The Toff was hardly able to get a word in. On his mind was the realization that Crossfield was playing for time. Vaguely he heard: *"My niece was with me when it started. I sent her out for help. Don't lose sight of him for a moment,*

178

officer." There was a lot more, lie upon lie upon lie. Crossfield was even lying when there seemed to be no need to. He talked as if Mary had been there from the beginning of it. He was protecting himself, and his niece.

From what?

The policeman tried to stem the words.

"Don't you worry, sir, I'll –"

"I've never seen anything like it in my life! He went mad. Absolutely mad!"

Rollison drew a deep breath, and when he spoke his voice was loud enough to drown Crossfield's, to startle the policeman and the man in shirt-sleeves.

"Keep quiet, Crossfield!"

"I –"

Rollison managed to keep hs voice high.

"I'm Rollison – understand? The Toff. Don't let the man or the woman out of your sight. They're both –"

Then Mary turned towards the door, and tried to get away. It was a foolish thing to do, for it confirmed the Toff's warning, and it gave the lie to Crossfield. The man in shirt-sleeves grabbed at Mary, while the policeman was gradually realizing what Rollison had said: "The Toff" did not fall strangely on the ears of London policemen.

Crossfield hesitated, and then said stiffly.

"Constable, I have warned you of the importance of seeing that this man is not allowed to go free."

"Never intended he should go free," said the policeman stolidly. "Nor *any* one in this flat, sir. Not until the C.I.D. men 'ave come, anyhow."

"My name is Crossfield, Arnold Crossfield, of the Crossfield Manufacturing Company." Crossfield rightly believed that would cause a stir, and some degree of deference. "I have an urgent appointment, and when I have attended to it I will gladly put myself at the disposal of the police."

179

"I –"

"Why did his niece try to run?" croaked Rollison.

Crossfield flashed:

"She has been badly frightened by this alarming show of violence." He was not giving in without a fight, although the Toff was vague about his real purpose. "Constable, you saw this man with the gun in his hand."

"I know, but –"

"Stop this – cackle," said the Toff with difficulty. "Wait for the Yard, Constable."

He was afraid that Crossfield would contrive to win a respite, but his anxiety disappeared when another shadow darkened the doorway – and yet another. He saw Inspector Bright of the Surrey C.I.D., with a burly man whom he knew well as Chief Inspector McNab, of Scotland Yard. Afterwards he was told that they had come to see Iris Brent, for Bright had not accepted her story on its face value, and had been prevented from acting as he would have liked by the Toff's apparent identification of her. That was a point which he and the Toff argued later at some length.

At that moment:

"What the devil's all this?" demanded Bright.

The words were hardly out of his mouth when Crossfield stepped back into the bedroom, and slammed the door. The movement was so unexpected that it flabbergasted the police for some seconds and they heard the key turn in the lock on the inside. Then the constable and Bright launched themselves against the door, thudding on it three times before it broke down.

The man in shirt-sleeves kept a firm hold on Mary.

Bright was into the room first, and past him Rollison saw Crossfield bending over the fireplace; he had a box of matches in his hand, and flames were blazing in the hearth. Rollison shouted:

"Put them out!"

The words were hardly necessary, for Bright was neither a fool nor slow to act. He stamped out the flames, which had only just caught the heap of papers which Crossfield had put into the grate, while the constable took Crossfield's right arm and maintained an uncompromising grip.

Rollison took all this in, and then began to slide down the wall. He could not keep his legs steady for another second. He did see Lossen's face, livid in its anger, before he lost consciousness, but he did not hear the exclamations of alarm from the others.

*

He was in hospital when he came round.

That was three hours afterwards; and another twelve passed before he saw anyone but Jolly and Moira Defoe. Both visited him in the small private ward, both declared they had no idea what the police were doing. Lett did not come to the hospital; Jolly gave the impression that he was following the case for the *Echo* and was afraid to let anything slip.

Moira said little, except that she had two invalids to visit, and she hoped the Toff would soon reduce that number to one. That was what he wanted to hear, and while he lay in bed, impatient at times but resigned at others because he could not be in for the final kill, he thought a great deal of the Defoes. Pat Defoe was a tempestuous individual, thoughtlessly selfish, seldom able to see more than his own point of view. As far as Moira was concerned he would surely grow out of that.

Defoe's part in the affair, so simply explained, was laughable.

Lossen's was almost understandable; a man of strange passions, of almost unnatural powers of hatred – a queer personality and one who would surely never be fully under-

181

stood. (Actually Rollison later spent some weeks trying to trace Lossen's ancestry, but failed. He did see the school-master, Nye, who confirmed that the man had been a phenomenon in his schooldays, always possessing a streak of cruelty; he had never let bygones be bygones but seemed driven to obtain satisfaction for the smallest slight. He also discovered more of Lossen's activities in America, and how he had contacted with Ma Parker when he had returned, for he had known of her son and the son's probable willing-ness to help him. Leslie Parker had helped him build the small but highly efficient gang. By the time the Toff made those inquiries, however, Lossen was awaiting trial, as were Parker and the other men, the Morris driver and the mechanic. The garage was owned by Lossen who had bought it nearly six months before.)

Iris Brent's part was also understandable.

She had had the one ambition; wealth, riches, luxury. She had met Lossen in America, and been fascinated by his money, but the gangster element had frightened her, and she had returned to England. There she had consorted with Crossfield, as she had done before her trip to the States.

A fickle, heartless woman, Rollison reflected; he disliked her more even than he did Lossen, who at least had some motive other than gain. The incident – to her it was no more – with Defoe had been actuated solely by the desire to squeeze every penny she could out of him, and thus she had contributed to the peculiarities of the case.

The Defoes . . .

Rollison would be at that stage in his thoughts – reflecting that Iris had made a bad bargain when she had thought to coerce Pat Defoe into paying blackmail – when he would think of Mary Crossfield, and his impatience would revive, he would make himself a nuisance to the nurses and the other staff; but no police visited him, and Lett stayed away.

On the second day Jolly told him that Defoe was quite all right, and on the road to recovery. Moira spent most of her time at the nursing-home, and Jolly no longer referred to her as "your young woman". Jolly told him also that Bill Crossfield was likely to be on his feet within three or four days, and was back at the Hall, with his mother.

But Mary – there was no news of Mary's part in the affair.

Or of the papers that Crossfield had tried to burn.

Would the police have some of their own back and keep those essential answers from him?

On the morning of the third day, when Rollison felt well enough to get up, although doctors and nurses pleaded with him to stay in bed, he told them that if either Bright or McNab, of the Yard, was not here by midday, he would go to the Yard and chance a relapse.

Nor did he think it was entirely a coincidence that on the stroke of twelve the door opened, and a nurse ushered in the Guildford inspector. Bright was smiling a little grimly as he shook hands, and sat down.

"Well, Mr. Rollison, you're anxious for a word with me, I'm told. It's rather a pity you didn't confide earlier, don't you think?"

Rollison lay back on his pillows.

"I do not," he said firmly. "There were too many things which could have gone wrong. Had I told you of Moira Defoe's presence – I didn't know her real name, anyhow – you would have been hot on the wrong trail, and many things might have happened which we would all regret. But I'm not pleading, Inspector! I'm asking for the information I would have got for myself had I been conscious another two or three hours. Crossfield's papers – what were they?

Bright smoothed his coat lapel.

"There's no reason why you shouldn't know – it will all come out in the trial."

"No reason why *I* shouldn't know!" gasped the Toff. "I – oh, all right, Bright, have it your own way. I'm still a sick man, but if any more crime crops up in your area I'll lead you a dance you won't forget in a hurry."

Bright laughed.

"I suppose you'd try! Actually" – he hedged his chair a little nearer – "I hope we wouldn't work at cross-purposes again. I suppose you've been making guesses?"

The Toff said very quickly:

"I've guessed a lot, and inferred a lot. I know Crossfield was out to cheat his nephew, I know that Lossen wanted to put the screw on him. I know all the minor details, and I suppose Mary Crossfield was in it somewhere. But I can't see how she would benefit –"

Bright raised a hand.

"That's the thing you missed all along, if you don't mind me reminding you." He was taking considerable pleasure in tantalizing the Toff, and the stiffness of his words made that more obvious. Rollison relaxed a little; the story would come. "It was the first essential," went on Bright. "You knew that Crossfield wanted full control of his companies, that Bill Crossfield had a substantial percentage, and he wanted his nephew to get out of his own free will. He needed help; he got it from the girl, who helped to work young Crossfield into a state of mind tempestuous enough to throw up his hand."

Rollison said very slowly:

"Well, well, well. And there were a dozen things which should have told me that while I was at the Hall."

"I thought you would realize it," said Bright smugly. "You missed an essential, as I've said."

"That's right, be wise after the event. What was her general scheme? In line with her uncle's?"

"Oh yes, they worked together. With young Mr. Cross-

184

field out of the running, they could have the companies between them. A very shrewd young woman, and her sole motive one of gain. So was Arnold Crossfield's of course."

"Gain and power," remarked the Toff.

"Ye-es. Well, as you learned, Defoe had some papers which would have broken the scheme. There were others. Crossfield knew nothing of the Iris Brent–Lossen association, and for safety's sake left them at the Brent woman's flat. Crossfield, his niece, and Iris Brent discussed details there, all with the sole idea of dispossessing William Crossfield. Lossen, of course, had regular reports of them. Crossfield wanted to get them away; even when he saw you and Lossen fighting he thought he could still succeed. Mary knew there was trouble, and came to get them in case he failed. They will convict both uncle and niece of trying to convert William Crossfield's fortune, or the bulk of it, to their own uses."

"It's not nice," said Rollison. "How is Bill?"

"He's done all he could to get Mary free, but the case is too strong –"

"If he doesn't make a charge, what will you do?"

"Oh, come," said Bright. "The Crossfields between them own most of the shares, but there are other shareholders, and it's a public liability company. Lossen will be charged with Iris Brent's murder, of course, and – but I won't weary you with the charges against the other people. You can guess most of them."

"Ye-es," admitted the Toff. "They're all guessable. I don't like the idea of Mary being on trial, but –"

"She and her uncle were both callous and unscrupulous," Bright said very formally. "They deserve no leniency. The other Crossfields will get over it, and I think Mr. William will take a much deeper interest in the business. If I may say so, Mr. Rollison, you are too much inclined to think of

185

individuals, and to ignore the social framework in which they work."

Rollison eyed him levelly.

"I wouldn't be surprised if you're right," he said. "I like people, even the little crooks. I even like some of the big ones. And as for the social framework –" He broke off, and smiled a little grimly. "I won't tell you what I think of it, Bright, it's so full of holes that individuals just can't help falling through it. Er – the Defoes are quite all right, aren't they?"

"I saw them just before coming here," said Bright. "They're guilty of nothing more than foolishness. Well, now, I must be going."

He stood up, and shook hands.

When he had gone, Rollison smiled. A worthy man, Bright, who would always work to the rigid rules of the community, framed for him in the Police Regulations. And that was no doubt as it should be. But what would have happened had he known a little of the truth before the duel with Lossen?

CHAPTER TWENTY-FIVE

Trial and After

THE Crossfield trial was one of the *cause célébrès* of the last few weeks of that summer. It took five days; and at the end of it Arnold Crossfield was convicted on a score of charges, for there was more motive behind his manipulations than the police had first suspected; the Toff's idea of "big things" was thoroughly vindicated. Crossfield had been amassing a large personal fortune by fraud and trickery within the companies which he had controlled in trust for Bill.

186

Throughout the trial it grew more and more obvious that Mary Crossfield had acted as a tool in her uncle's hands, and Rollison was not surprised to learn, on the final day, that she received no more than a "token" sentence of twelve months imprisonment. So the law studied the human angle and considered human frailties, which was what the Toff did above all other things.

Bill Crossfield was not at the trial except to give a little evidence on the third day; his mother did not appear at all.

It was in Lossen's trial that the Defoes figured most prominently. Lossen was sentenced to the full penalty of the law; his men to long terms of imprisonment. There was no angle of the affair not finally brought to the light of day, and it had not been a pleasant spell for the Defoes. But after it, they went to Rollison's flat, where Jolly admitted them. Lett was already there; by then he knew them well.

Moira looked years younger, thought the Toff; and Pat Defoe seemed to have shaken off the unpleasantness of the trial with no great effort.

He sat down, stretched his legs in front of him, and said:

"Well, thank the Lord it's over Rollison, I don't know where the devil Moira and I would have been if you hadn't come along. What *really* brought you?"

Rollison laughed.

"Your love for cricket," he said. "Your failure to turn up rang so false. And Wally Simm was loyalty itself."

Defoe smiled, contentedly.

"He always was. He was alone, I think, in knowing that there was a studio at the back of the garage. Er – we're going down there, Moira and I – London's a bit too sticky for us at the moment. Seriously, Rollison, we can't thank you enough. Everything else apart, if you hadn't turned up we would probably be living separately, and thinking darkly of each other."

187

"And that's only one thing," said Moira warmly. "If you hadn't been there, Iris would have cleared herself – I know she would."

Rollison smiled, and said :

"I don't know that you're right. The law's a queer thing, and the police work in weird and wonderful ways, at times, but they do get at the truth. The trouble is, they usually take so long, and while they're getting it tragedy's so often hovering near. But they have to work to the rules, they can't take chances. Had Bright seen you instead of me, you would have gone to the station for questioning, he couldn't have taken the chance that you were innocent of everything because he liked the look of your eyes."

"Oi!" cried Defoe.

"That's enough from you," said Rollison amiably. He was in a mood to talk, and he told them much of his theory of life, of his reason for spending so much time in the East End, of his conviction that there would always be room for a man, or for men, who would take the law in their own hands, not to break it but to help to conserve it.

As he talked, Jolly prepared dinner.

While it was being served, a car drew up outside, and when the Toff looked out of the window he stared in amazement, and then called the others hastily. They craned their necks to see Dr. Whittaker of Fern Cross standing by the open door of his car, and Wally Simm climbing out of it. Soon afterwards they heard the others climbing the stairs, and when they were admitted Wally complained bitterly of "them things", by which he meant cars of all description. Since his part in the affair had been hidden as much as possible, and since Iris Brent had not lived to be tried, he had not been called for testimony. But he had prevailed on the doctor to drive him to London and to hear part of the trial, and then to visit the Toff.

So Jolly stretched a meal for four to feed a party of six, and Wally Simm in his low-pitched and monotonous voice told the company that he had always thought Mr. Defoe a real gentleman, and had "never took heed" of what was said about him. And he had always hoped he and his wife would get together again.

That remark brought a short tense silence.

"But" – Defoe broke it – "*you* didn't know I was married."

"Don't you believe it," said Wally Simm dourly. "I weren't deceived, not Wally Simm. All the time in your workshop there was a photygraph – from your wife, it said on the back, I read it. "Some day she'll come back,' I said to meself, and the day I set eyes on her at the cottage 'fore that other woman came, I thought it would be all right."

Rollison said weakly:

"You – you *saw* her?"

"I looked in just afore the match," declared Wally. "So I see her then, an' I thought it would be all right. That's why I was so mighty anxious to go and see – I thought you'd be as happy as sandboys, and instead – well, all's well that ends well, don't they say?"

He was a little morose for a while after that, for he could not understand what amused the Toff so much.